BOUND AND BEWITCHED

WREN CARTWRIGHT

Content Notes

Please be aware that the content in this book may not be suitable for all readers

The warnings are as follows:

- Death of a parent (past, mentioned)
- Mild bullying
- Mentions and brief descriptions of past illness
- Sexually explicit content

Due to the list above, reader discretion is advised.

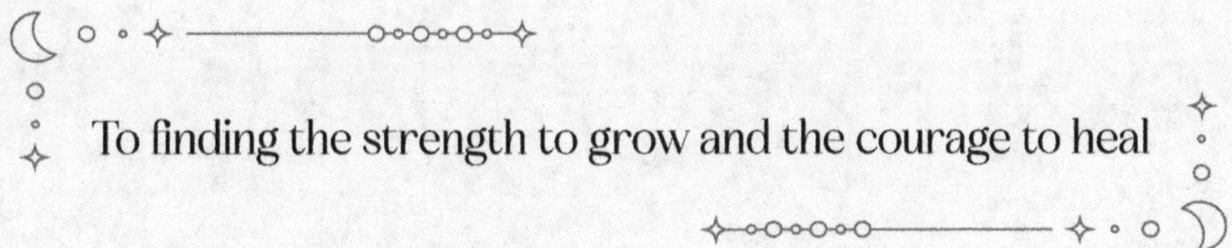

To finding the strength to grow and the courage to heal

"And forget not that the earth delights to feel your bare feet and the winds long to play with your hair."

— KHALIL GIBRAN

Chapter 1

Sᴜɴʟɪɢʜᴛ sᴛʀᴇᴀᴍᴇᴅ ᴛʜʀᴏᴜɢʜ ᴛʜᴇ small, diamond-paned windows, casting golden hues across the worn wooden floorboards. The crackling fire in the hearth filled the room with a comforting warmth, chasing away the chill from the midmorning. I hummed as I worked, the bowl in my hands cool and smooth, covered in hand-painted flowers by my niece—her gift to me last winter solstice. Items made with love were always so much better than anything I could purchase for myself. The river rock nestled inside set off the blue shades nicely; a dark gray color patterned with whorls of ivory that I'd found on the river bank and pocketed for Litharos. He loved pretty stones, which was fitting for the god of the rivers and small streams. A whispered spell, and the embedded dirt had sloughed right off. It was a simple incantation, but especially useful for minor things, and one of the first my mother had taught me. I set the bowl back onto his altar and brushed my hands together before propping them on my hips.

While I had an overwhelming list of tasks to complete on any given day, keeping them organized was beyond me. My sisters often teased me for my scattered schedule, though I put my foot down when they tried to get me to use someone from the village. The humiliation was simply not worth it. My best friend, Esmeraude, laughed every time she heard the rumors they'd come up with for me, although it was rare they slipped up around her nowadays; everyone knew that after her disbelieving laughter came the lecture of a lifetime. One of the few not intimidated by me, we'd been fast friends ever since we'd spent the day playing together as children while my mother prepared a tonic for her ill grandfather. Esme would probably help if I asked it of her, but she had her own responsibilities. Her days were filled with working for her parents at the fromagerie they owned.

Silas rubbed against my ankles with a low purr, then jumped onto the cluttered windowsill to watch the bird that had just landed on a low-hanging branch of the tree out front—a majestic oak that turned vibrant in the fall and was a skeletal masterpiece in the winter. He would spend all his time in the windowsill if he could, sunning his black fur and watching the wildlife.

A knock sounded at the door, and my skirt swished around my calves as I crossed the room to open it.

"Isolde!"

My sister grinned, but she couldn't hold the expression very long and it fell seconds later, leaving behind her usual unruffled mask. The older she got, the more she resembled our father. They shared the same cornflower-blue eyes and dark-blonde hair, with a button nose and thin face, as did Isadora—our youngest sister. I, on the other hand, had received our mother's short stature, pale-green eyes, and dark brown hair that held the white streak of a witch near my temple. The similarities between the two of them stopped there, though. Where my father was generous with his affection, my sister was almost brittle with her reserve.

I pulled her into a quick embrace, keeping clear of the cane resting at her side and noting how she clutched briefly at the back of my shirt, then ushered her into the warm room once she let go. The worried fidgeting of her hands didn't escape my notice. My sister was a practical woman, and I could count on one hand the amount of times I'd seen her truly unsettled.

"Is it your knee? I have some more of that salve—"

She cut me off with a sweep of her hand, looking immeasurably tired as she sank into one of the intricately carved wooden chairs at my round table. The set had been a birthday gift from my father several years back. My cottage was filled with reminders of my family, from the pale-yellow drapes my younger sister had embroidered to the unfinished artwork sketched on my kitchen windowsill after Isolde had overindulged one night.

"Have you heard from Father?" she asked. Fear turned my blood to ice, and whatever expression my face had frozen in made her rush to clarify. "No, no, he's okay. Just... Have you spoken?"

"No." I leaned back against the counter, heart still racing. Our mother had passed too soon, and it was an unshakeable fear some nights that our father would as well. He'd been sick last year—really sick—and it had been a miracle when he'd recovered. Same with Callum, Isa's son. "Why?"

Isolde took a deep breath, then exhaled it in a huff. "I think something's wrong." I opened my mouth, but she held up a staying hand. "*Not* with his health. He was just acting... odd when I visited him last."

"Has Isa mentioned anything?" She only lived several doors down from my father and saw him the most often.

"Nothing. She said he's been acting a little differently, but anytime she tried to pry, he changed the subject. Something about treats for the kids."

Which wouldn't have been hard. My niece and nephew were forces of nature who loved their grandfather dearly. They could easily be the stars of an hour-long conversation, especially when plied with sweets.

"You want me to visit him?"

It had been at least several weeks since we'd last seen one another, as he'd been occupied looking after Isa's children while she worked on preparations for the upcoming Thaloria Festival.

"If you could. I'm sure he's fine, but…"

"I know." He was stubborn on the best of days and believed that all his problems should rest entirely on his shoulders. "I'll go tomorrow."

Isolde's shoulders dropped from where they hovered around her ears. "Thank you."

I studied my sister for a moment, grateful her attention was elsewhere as she watched Silas chirp at a bird perched in the tree. The shadows under her eyes had deepened since I saw her last, and she rubbed absently at her knee. It was an old injury, the result of a fall when climbing a tree to try saving one of the village's few stray cats when we were in our early teens. After the incident, she'd become almost unrecognizable. Once the most adventurous of us all, she instead spent her days at home and shadowed our father as he worked. Despite all our attempts to care for the injury as best we could, her knee had never healed quite right. After mother had passed, I took over brewing tonics and salves to ease her pain.

"Here," I said, grabbing a few tins from the antique cabinet where I stored all my creations. I placed them in a small, linen bag and set it on the table in front of her.

She shook her head, about to protest, when I stopped her. "Take them, please. They're going unused, and I made them specially for you. Use them or don't, but they're yours." Another thought hit me, and I paused. "They haven't stopped working, have they?"

"No." Isolde sighed as she slumped. "I just... ran out."

I couldn't force Isolde to come to me when she needed more, so it seemed I'd need to make more regular trips to see her.

The items in the bag *clinked* together as she lifted it, pushing herself to a stand. "Tomorrow, yes? You promise?"

"I promise."

Chapter 2

MAMA CRACKED THE GRIMOIRE *open, running her finger down the yellowed pages. "All the witches before you in our line have honored him," she said. "And you will continue the tradition."*

Some of her most requested stories when I was young were about the temples scattered across our more sacred cities, where the gods were praised and worshiped daily by thousands of people—not just witches, but anyone. How in these cities, magic was used liberally, and the arcane arts were commonplace. We might've settled in such a place if she hadn't found Father here. He had no desire to leave, as he'd lived his entire life in this village and wanted his children to do the same.

Sometimes I resented him for the whispers I'd heard when I was younger. Isolde and Isa never had to hear such things. They weren't born with magic like I'd been and had left me to be the sole keeper of my mother's knowledge and all those who came before her. According to my mother, plenty of witches practiced with little to no generational magic, but no matter how often she'd encouraged my sisters to join us for lessons, they'd refused.

Still, it was a path I'd wanted to pursue. I laid my head on her arm, watching as she traced the edges of the grimoire, just like when I was a child. It wasn't hers, but our family's that had been passed down. Our line was fairly eclectic in their beliefs and paths, save for our patron god, Thorne.

Mama had a whole host of other deities she worked with—and predicted that I would one day have the same—but he was one that had continued throughout generations. The god of cleverness and trickery, justice and broken oaths; revered for his arbitrations, feared for his mischievous side. A minor god, like his twin, but no less powerful. I asked her once why we'd worshiped him for so long, and her only answer was that he'd done our family a great service in the past.

"It's time," she whispered. The fire crackled across from us, casting moving shadows throughout the cozy room. Golden threads glowed in the tapestries that lined the walls, and faint remnants of smoke curled lazily about the room. I was glad Papa had taken my sisters out for the evening, grateful to have quiet time. My celebration earlier had been loud, likely overcompensating for the lack of attendance, but I'd preferred it that way. Just my family and Esme. I'd even spotted a purple-breasted silverwing that morning. The violet, shimmering

bird was so rare that it was almost certainly a gift from Deeara, the goddess of wisdom and hunting.

"Eight and ten years, my dear girl. Are you ready to learn more about your heritage? To make your first offering?"

I nodded, staring avidly at the familiar book. All the witches in my family had waited until this age to truly start deity work. It was too important an undertaking to treat with anything other than the reverence and maturity that came with time. Not all gods would let flippancy from a child innocently pass without consequences.

The candles on the mantle flickered wildly, and the scent of oranges from our tree outside wafted in on the breeze.

"I'm ready," I said, tracing the section on divinations, the antique paper crackling under my fingertip.

THE DOOR SWUNG OPEN at my knock, and a sense of foreboding washed over me. I was only a few steps past the entryway when I heard a deep huff come from the kitchen. I dropped the woven basket I'd brought and dashed across the house, worried my father had hurt himself, or worse.

I found him sitting at the table, shoulders slumped and face drawn. He jolted as I entered the room, watery, red-rimmed eyes landing on me. "Elisette? Why are you here?"

What could possibly be wrong? I tried to recall if there were any anniversaries for this month, but came up with nothing. "Are you alright?"

"I'm fine. You should go," he said, gesturing toward the front of the house with a firm nod. My head spun as I tried to figure out what could possibly be wrong. Retreating from the room to grab the basket I'd dropped, I just barely overheard his relieved sigh.

My walk back was slower, noticing the unusual disarray that I'd missed in my rush to get to him. Blankets, pillows, and clothes lay haphazardly around the floor of the small, cozy living room, pictures hung askew, and the stool that normally sat beside the fireplace had been overturned. I marched back into the kitchen with renewed purpose, ignoring his groan when he realized I had no intention of leaving.

"What's wrong?" I asked—well, demanded really—fingers clutching at the locket my mother had given me for strength.

He shook his head. It was exasperating how his stubbornness sometimes rivaled Isolde's. Deep grooves lined his aging face, creases forming at the corners of his eyes and lines framing his mouth. It struck me every now and then just how quickly he was aging. Sometimes it felt like no time had passed at all since we were children, and others, it was all too apparent. I softened my approach, reaching out to rest a hand over his where it lay on the wooden tabletop. "Please? We're worried about you."

"Bah, I should've known Isolde would go to you. She looked far too suspicious on her last visit."

"For good reason," I scolded. "Now tell me."

"My girls," he whispered. "We did a good job with you." Before I could respond, he withdrew his hand—not without giving mine a firm squeeze first—and leaned back in his chair. "I'm going to sell the house and land, as well as a considerable chunk of my belongings. I have maybe a month left with everything."

Shock held my tongue captive as I thought of all that could mean. He'd lived here practically his entire life, moving in after he married Mama and raising us in these familiar halls. All our memories... The scuffed corner on the mantle where Isolde had thrown the poker once after a fit, the hand-painted stars on the cabinets behind me from when Isa had started an art class at school and thought they needed to be prettier, and the many tiny wooden embellishments Mama had added to every surface throughout the years. It had been a tight fit for all five of us, almost too tight at times, but it was home.

"You... you can't," I stuttered.

"No choice to it, dearest. Besides, maybe it's time, hmm?"

"It's only time if you decide it's time. Why don't you have a choice? What's going on?"

He hung his head, knotted fingers tracing the scratches in the tabletop. "I have debts."

"Debts?" My father was not a betting man. Besides, he'd given up woodworking when his hands grew too stiff to manipulate his tools, but he still had a good few pieces he could sell off for a decent profit if he was in trouble.

"You can't breathe a word of this to anyone. Do you understand?" When I reluctantly nodded, he continued, "It wasn't by chance that Callum recovered last year. I might've slowly improved, but Callum was only getting worse. He was too young to handle such an illness, and it was going to kill him."

Memories flew by of late nights spent making restorative soups to boost his energy and cold compresses to try breaking his fever. The heavy scents of menthol and ginger that had filled the kitchen from various tonics and blends to help him breathe easier. Isa had been beside herself, so Isolde and I had moved in to help care for them both around the clock. It was a wonder her daughter, Callista, hadn't fallen ill as well.

"What are you saying? You did something to help him?"

"Ah, Elise. He was so thin, barely even conscious for more than a few minutes at a time. There was a man in the village selling medicines. A doctor. He was just passing through for the day, following the trade routes west. I couldn't... I couldn't afford it, so I went down to the council and begged for a loan."

"We could've helped! We still can help. It can't have been that bad."

My father gave a deep sigh, rubbing a hand down his face. "Maybe. Maybe if I'd swallowed my pride in the beginning and just asked for help. But Isa is already struggling to get by with what Finn can send home, and you and Isolde don't have an excess by any means. The problem is that everything the council had offered would've taken days. Alden... He'd made me an offer on the spot straight from his own coffers. There would be a hefty fee for the short notice and for each day it took me to repay him, but I'd have a means of paying the doctor right away. I knew I could worry about everything else later. And it worked! Callum drank the entire bottle and was more alert the next day than he'd been in weeks."

"Alden?! That man has swindled more people than I can count, and we can't even do anything about it just because his parents invested so much into the village." My stomach twisted just picturing him with his too-blond hair and fake smile preying on my family's misfortune.

"It's my duty as a father and grandfather to take on any burdens I know you cannot carry. The loan has since far exceeded its initial sum, but I have it under control. The land and house should cover it with enough left over for me to settle somewhere modest."

I rubbed at my chest, where a dull ache had formed. "You can't sell. I won't allow it."

A raised eyebrow had me sinking deeper into my chair.

"I won't," I mumbled, glancing into the other room. "And that mess in there, is that related to this?"

He laughed. "That bad? I just... I've been too overwhelmed to keep up with things around here."

"There has to be something we can do. This is your *home*."

"Things change, sweetheart. That's life."

"Not this." I stood so quickly that my chair teetered.

Chapter 3

Sunlight streamed through the window, *bringing some color back to Mama's face. The air was filled with the comforting scent of chamomile, and the fainter, cloying odor of sickness and peppermint.*

Mama watched me pace from where she lay in bed. Thick, wavy brown hair so similar to mine stood out against the cream-colored pillow where it was spread. The unique lock of white hair that we shared had turned a muted grey shade, and currently lay tangled with the other strands. Her face was pale and drawn, but her eyes still held their sparkle as she beckoned me closer. With trembling hands, she reached behind her neck to unclasp the chain there.

"Elise, my dear," she said softly, her voice barely above a whisper. "I want you to have this."

I glanced down at the locket as she dropped it into my open palms, my heart pounding in my chest. It was a beautiful piece of jewelry, engraved with fine-lined, swirling patterns. It gleamed in the sunlight, its scratched and golden surface reflecting years of use.

"But Mama," I protested, my voice catching in my throat. "It's yours. You should keep it." There wasn't a day she'd not worn the familiar necklace. She would need it, wouldn't she? She'd wear it for many years to come.

She smiled weakly, her hand reaching out to touch mine. "It's time, Elise. It's yours now. Besides, this necklace has been in our family for generations. We're just a little more ahead of schedule than we thought we'd be."

Tears pricked at the corners of my eyes as I traced the designs on the locket's surface with a gentle touch. "You've never opened it?"

Her head shook slowly, so as not to worsen her headache. "Can't be opened."

I sniffled, fastening the chain around my neck. The weight of the locket against my chest felt familiar, as if it had always been there. "Maybe if... I'll give it back. When you're better."

"If I get better, daughter of mine, I will gladly accept it back."

IT WASN'T OFTEN THAT I ever purposely walked around the village. I wasn't inherently shy, but it was easier to stick to the shadows, taking my time so my clumsiness didn't cause any accidents that would surely draw more negative attention. The stares just proved that I was right to. My reputation preceded me. Except, of course, if someone was ill or injured. Then the villagers would reluctantly brave the deep, dark woods to get to my cottage, making sure to avoid the pit of snakes out front and hoping I didn't send them home with a curse. Except that the forest was filled with life and light, and my home was a welcoming, warm space. Not to mention, I'd never seen a snake at all past the age of eight, when Isolde and I would dig in the garden beds and Isa would yell at us for scaring her with them.

All around me, conversation hushed as I hurried down the cobblestone streets, admiring the quaint, rustic buildings on either side that I so rarely got to see with my head tucked into the hood of my cloak. I supposed that didn't help my clumsiness either.

Our village was made up of sloping roofs and stone buildings, with arcane lanterns lining the streets every so often. The village had learned its lesson in using old-fashioned lit torches after several buildings burned down years prior due to an unfortunate incident with an agitated horse. Of course, they had no issue trading with the larger towns and guilds for magic when it was convenient to them. It's not that they hated anything magic, they just... preferred to go without it. Like their issue with torches, one bad experience in the past had tainted their perception of witches for decades.

The rich scents of yeast and spices drifted from the bakery that made the most delicious walnut bread—I only ate it when Isa had time to bring by a basket—and laughter spilled out from the tavern on the corner. I could see people moving inside Esmeraude's shop, pointing at the items on display, but I had no time to stop in and greet her.

The further I ventured into the village, the louder it grew. My sisters would be here if they could, but my father was right: I didn't want to upset them with a burden they could do nothing about. They had social standing here—lives and jobs and goodwill. I had nothing but time and the freedom to explore all avenues; it made sense that I would do it myself. Besides, I'd sworn not to tell. Although, I knew if it came down to it, I would. My bond with my sisters was unbreakable, and that included secrets.

The council building loomed up ahead, its charming ironwork giving a deceptive impression of the welcome I knew I'd find. My head throbbed, and I spared a hand to rub my forehead, trying to smooth out the ache. I'd spent the entire night thinking of possible solutions for my father. I had nothing of worth to sell—most of my belongings were of sentimental value, not monetary—and even if I sold off my entire inventory, it wouldn't come close to the number he'd named. I already knew my sisters didn't have the funds needed. Isolde lived comfortably, but frugally, and Isa's husband worked at the docks, frequently leaving on the ships to the north. He sent everything he made back home to them, and it all went to their children.

My only option was the very solution my father had tried in the first place: the council. He was unable to borrow with the debt hanging over his head, Alden had made sure of that, but that didn't mean I couldn't.

The exterior of the building was devoid of people as I approached. I knocked lightly on the heavy wooden door, holding my breath as I waited for a response. A snicker sounded behind me, and my entire body tensed. *Is it too late to try something else?*

Someone called faintly for me to come in. I stumbled slightly as I entered, grateful I'd chosen to wear trousers and not something I would trip over even more.

The collection of chairs near the far end, by the big, sweeping window that overlooked the street, was familiar to me. I'd been called here many times to defend something or other. Once, it was a mother who'd accused my itch-relieving cream of making her child sick, only to realize they'd eaten spoiled food earlier in the day. Or when I was brought before the council so they could convince me that my future lay elsewhere in a town that wasn't this one. Mother had been gone by then, or she wouldn't have stood for it. I had nothing but bad memories of this dated building and the old men who sat within. It was hard sometimes to be so ostracized, but it wasn't all bad. I had my magic, and my cottage, and the love of my family. Even better would be a child or student to pass my knowledge on to, but it seemed that wouldn't happen for me in this lifetime. I was officially a spinster, and I'd yet to have any desire to tie myself to anyone. No, I would just write everything down in my grimoires as my family had for centuries, then pass them off to whoever would care for them best until someone else came along who wanted to learn from them. Maybe Callista; that girl would outlive us all.

Fernando, the head of the council, sighed as I approached. "Elisette. So nice to see you here." His coat bunched as he sat, and he still somehow looked down his nose at me despite being half my height. His golden-brown skin appeared muted in the building, even with the sunlight streaming in. Like the structure itself was feeding off of everyone's misery and doubling it.

If I wasn't trying to appeal to them, I'd consider speaking my mind, but I couldn't risk it. Instead, I took a deep breath in and tried to focus my thoughts. It was embarrassing how many times I'd practiced what I was going to say, yet I couldn't seem to find the words.

All faces turned toward the elaborate door at the back of the room, offering miniscule nods to... *Damn.*

"Alden."

"Lissy." Alden greeted me with an ever-widening grin. I didn't bother to correct him. He only called me Lissy because he knew it bothered me, and rewarding it with attention meant he would never stop. He wore his usual elaborate clothing—bright colors and coarse fabrics—giving him the impression of a visiting merchant instead of someone who lived here. His gaze swept my body, and I noticed his smile dim when he reached my pants. Of course, they would bother him; he liked his women demure and delicate, bundled in elaborate skirts that made them look a spectacle when he paraded them throughout the village.

He took the empty seat closest to me and settled in to watch the show. I'd assumed his absence meant I would have an easier time pleading my case. I should have known there was no way he would miss this.

"Good, well... I-I've come today because I—"

Alden held up a hand to halt my stuttering. "This is about your father, yes?"

"Yes," I said through gritted teeth.

He turned to address the room. "I'm sure you remember when John came to make his request. Out of the goodness of my heart, I gave him exactly what he needed once I realized he needed an immediate solution."

The frown Fernando suppressed at his words told me all I needed to know. Clearly, I wasn't the only one who couldn't stand the insufferable man in front of me. "I wasn't aware of this," he huffed.

"We've spoken about this before—you using your own resources to make offers to every soul we turn down."

Alden shrugged. "I am, first and foremost, a businessman."

Heads turned as Fernando muttered something unsavory under his breath. "Be that as it may," he responded, visibly taking deep, calming breaths, "we're the ones who end up handling the inevitable disputes and complaints. Maybe you might consider that next time."

Clearing my throat to draw their attention, I tried not to tap my foot as I waited for them to face me. "Yes," I started. "Lovely as this whole operation is, I could use your assistance."

The man to Alden's right sighed. I had to actively meet his eyes rather than gawk at the white beard that grew all the way to his stomach. "If what Alden says is true..." He looked to me for confirmation and when I nodded, he continued, "There's nothing we can do."

They wouldn't say it, but I knew. Alden *was* the council. Fernando might hold the title, but Alden held too much influence and had too much of a monetary stake to not be heavily involved in their decisions. In his opinion, it would make no sense for him to agree to allocate funds or support to the very man he'd put in this position.

Something in my chest burned as I struggled not to make a scene. "There must be *something* you can do."

"I'm afraid not," Fernando added quietly, hands clasped in his lap.

"I could work for it. I... I can offer my services. It's almost the season for spring fever, and you could use my help with remedies and care. There must be something." I coughed to hide the strain that started to creep into my words and tucked my hands behind my back to hide their trembling. I wished Silas were with me, but knew he most likely wouldn't have been allowed inside despite being better behaved than half the men here. "Why would you even have him here when he's the reason multiple people are in the same situation as my father?" I asked as I flung out my arm toward Alden. Immediately after I said it, I knew I'd fucked up. We all knew why he was there; he relished the control, the status. They would never turn someone with such a far-reaching and well-off family away.

No one answered, instead exchanging looks varying from sheepish to irritated.

It had been so many moons since I'd last felt the desperate, clawing ache of hopelessness that its return stole my breath. I'd pinned everything on the council being helpful in some fashion. That they had nothing at all to offer was... devastating.

I walked out of the building in a daze, ignoring the mumbled apologies and half-hearted attempts to console me. The scents from the bakery on the corner reached me once more, yet this time all I could think about was the strange looks I would receive if I tried to walk in and purchase something. I was feared because I held myself apart, and I held myself apart because I was feared. The isolation was crushing.

Someone grabbed me, and noise flooded back in—shopkeepers advertising their wares, an older woman chastising the man at her side, and a group of giggling children playing games with stones beside one of the fruit stalls. I looked up into the calculating blue eyes of none other than the man I'd just fled from and yanked my arm from his hold.

"Easy," he cautioned. His grip left behind reddened fingerprints on my otherwise pale skin, and I rubbed my other hand over them like I could soothe them away.

"Haven't you done enough?" I admonished.

I turned on my heel to leave when his voice cut through the chatter. "I might have a solution to your problem." *Vesta give me strength...* He raised a brow at my crossed arms but seemed satisfied enough that I was no longer trying to leave. "I'm in need of something... rare."

"Why should I care?"

"*Because*," he said, drawing out the word like maybe I hadn't heard him properly, "Maybe we could come to an agreement."

"Fine. What is it you want?"

Alden lowered his voice just enough that those around us wouldn't be able to overhear his next word. "Vitalara."

"Vitalara," I repeated slowly. "Absolutely not!" The vitalara plant was arcane in nature, fabled to eradicate illnesses like no other modern medicine or herb, but incredibly temperamental. Only someone with magic could prepare it in just the right way to activate its properties. It was rumored to be extinct. Finding it was a joke. Impossible.

Alden was mortified at the rise in volume. "Yes," he hissed, gaze darting toward our onlookers. He took hold of my arm once more, this time gentler, and tugged me into the shade of a nearby shop that had already closed for the day. "Just listen, Elisette. You're not the only one who's had sick family. My mother is ill, and her condition is worsening by the day. I throw gold around, and nothing happens. I use my influence, and they tell me reputation won't bring a missing plant back from the dead. You're my last hope. You must have... *witchy* connections."

Did he think I was in contact with every witch around the world? That I spoke to them at night through my mirror while we cursed people we didn't like for fun? "You would ask the same person you've ridiculed for years? Is this a joke?"

He hesitated, and when I made a move to back away, he huffed. "Fine! Fine. I'll clear your father's debt. *All* of it."

Shock and indecision kept me from immediately shouting out my agreement. Where would you even start looking for something that in all likelihood didn't exist anymore? I raised my chin, fixing him with a bold stare and hoping he wouldn't catch on to the fact that I was using every muscle I possessed and then some to pretend like I had any power in this situation. The more confident I appeared, the better. "Not only do I want my father's debt forgiven, but an extra finder's fee for the trouble. And I want five weeks to try to procure it. If I fail... I will take over the balance he owes."

A blond, skeptical brow arched high. He was right to be hesitant; I had no idea what I would do if I failed. It wasn't like I could pull the money out from under my mattress, and gods knew he would do something underhanded like double the amount for wasting his time. "Four weeks with an added fee if you fail to follow through. I fear my mother doesn't have very long."

My palms ached from being curled too tight, and I knew when I opened them there would be imprints left in my skin from my nails. What would Isolde do? She's the shrewd one, always negotiating on our behalf. I tried to bargain once, but ended up paying twice the original amount. Alden shifted impatiently, and I realized there wasn't much of a choice to it at all. I'd do anything to help my family.

"I'll do it."

The sly, pleased grin I received in return should've worried me, and it did, a little. But I was still flooded with relief at the chance that our childhood home and land would remain in the family, and that I had taken a tiny bit of control back. The panic would come later.

"Four weeks," he called out after me as I weaved my way through the small crowd that had gathered, desperate to get back to familiar surroundings.

Chapter 4

"Four weeks!" Esmeraude shouted, hands slamming down onto the table as she stared at me as though I possibly had another answer for her.

I sighed. "That's right." She seemed even taller than usual from where I was sprawled out against my overstuffed jewel-toned pillows, watching her pace. She hadn't sat once since storming in thirty minutes ago, going on about how everyone was gossiping about my trip into town yesterday and my mysterious talk with Alden.

She paused to pet Silas, serious brown eyes flashing behind her spectacles as she shot me an unhappy look. "I don't have a speck of magic to my name, and even *I* know how rare vitalara is. How do you ever plan to find it in time?"

"Esme..."

"You have no idea, do you?"

I could've pretended to have a plan. Faked the confidence I knew would put her at ease, at least for the moment, but it wouldn't come. "No. But I'll think of something."

Esme cocked her head toward the far wall where my altars were. "Can they help you?"

"These are mortal problems. They likely wouldn't know where to begin or have any interest."

She finally took a seat, the candlelight at the table flickering across her dark skin and giving her warm, gold highlights. "You need to tell your sisters."

"I can't. What could they possibly do? It would only disrupt their lives and worry them." I held up my hand when she opened her mouth to protest. "*Please* don't tell them. I promise that if there's any way they could possibly help me that I will let them know then. Otherwise, I'll keep it to myself."

"You'd probably have better luck coming up with the payment," she grumbled.

"It'll just take research. I'll start by seeing what I have in my books, then inquire around the village."

"I'll ask any merchants that pass through," Esme decided. She pushed her round spectacles up to rest higher on her nose, then sipped at the lemon-balm tea I'd made her. Her favorite drink of mine. It had a touch of luck added when brewing that she insisted tasted like sugared oranges, even though I'd assured her time and time again that you couldn't *taste* the magic.

Speaking of merchants... The festival might be a good place to question visitors. Maybe Esme might be free this year. She helped her parents hand out samples from their inventory late into the night, which meant I usually spent the celebration alone unless Isolde was feeling particularly charitable.

"Are you ready for the festival?"

That earned me an eye roll that I knew meant her parents had plans for her. "We're working with the baker next door to create a stall for those cheese puffs you love so much. I can only hope that next year they choose something easier to make so that my arms don't fall off before the festivities even begin."

I snickered, quickly masking it with a cough. Esme fixed me with a droll stare that caused another giggle to escape. Then, unable to help herself, she grinned back at me.

"You know I'd help you if I had any skill at baking whatsoever."

"I know." She snorted. "Remember the time you burnt that shortcake? Isa screamed like the entire house was going up in flames."

"It was just a little smoke," I huffed. "She's so dramatic."

"This is true. It's like your mother saved it all for her after giving you and Isolde so little."

I wrapped my fingers around the locket that hung from my neck, the metal warm from my skin. "Yeah. I suppose she did."

A STEADY STREAM OF smoke from the rosemary and cedar burning to my right wafted up my nose, making me cough uncontrollably over the book I was reading. Silas gave a disgruntled *mew* from where he was sprawled out beside my chair, and I realized once I glimpsed the darkness beyond my window that he'd probably been hungry for some time.

"Sorry." I sighed, clearing my throat one last time and massaging my temples before pushing my chair back. "Got caught up."

He trilled like he understood. I liked to think he did. We had our own language forged through years spent together, after all. Silas had come into my life over six years ago after I'd found him nestled up by a tree in the forest behind my home on a particularly dreary day.

I closed the book and drew the curtains. My gaze drifted to my mismatched furniture, each piece bearing the marks of time and love. A well-worn armchair sat by the window, its cushions passed down through generations and adorned with intricate needlework. Next to it, a sturdy oak table was cluttered with bundles of dried herbs and vials that I was still working with. In the corner, shelves overflowed with jars of ingredients, their labels faded with age but still legible. The air was heavy with the mingling scents of dried lavender, earthy sage, and the faint hint of spices.

What kind of place would my father move to if he sold the house? Would it be cozy like this? Filled with familiar objects and things that reminded him of my mother?

My stomach growled. "Alright, alright," I muttered, heading into the kitchen. After braiding my hair back from my face and wondering how I could possibly shed so many long, brown hairs daily without going bald, I dished up some bland pieces of the chicken I'd prepared earlier for Silas before adding seasoning, pine nuts, and roasted carrots to the side of mine. A whispered spell my mother had passed on from my grandmother reheated the tea that had begun to cool in my mug.

When the pillar candle at Thorne's altar snuffed out, I huffed. "You don't even like chicken, and I know for a fact that you can't stand carrots."

The cottage was silent aside from the small snarling noises Silas made as he ate beside me and the crackling from the hearth as a new log caught ablaze. Wind rattled against the old, glazed window, but a quick glance confirmed that it hadn't spontaneously shattered into pieces. Despite how many times Isolde told me that nothing short of a tree branch falling through it would break it, I still got nervous when the wind picked up. I turned my attention back to my meal, only to jump so high that my chair nearly flew back when a large piece of wood in the hearth tumbled into several lower pieces with a loud *crash*, sending embers and ash flying.

"Enough!" I exclaimed. "What could possibly be wrong?"

It took a fair amount of energy for the deities I worshiped to affect this realm. Their powers were restricted, mostly limited to observation and suggestion. Manifesting in dreams was a much more reliable way for them to communicate, as was symbolism. If they *really* wanted to, they could do more, but why would they?

The book I'd been reading earlier went flying from the table, landing open and face down on the floor. Anyone one who'd witnessed it would surely blame a specter, but I knew better. "That book is priceless! It's practically still bound just by hope alone." Every single candle in the room flickered wildly for a single second, and I stopped, finally realizing that something more was going on.

Picking it up gently, I examined the pages it landed open on. The edges were lined with some kind of dried substance, indicating that they'd been stuck together for some time before being pried open now. The first image caught my eye from where it sat illustrated in dreamy watercolors in the upper left. I recognized that face... I'd seen a different rendering of her over a decade ago, on the page opposite her twin as my mother introduced our patron god to me.

She was hauntingly beautiful, painted with faded silvers and pinks like the princesses in my storybooks when I was a child. Sylvane was her name. The goddess of wheat and bountiful harvests; of abundance and goodwill.

Why did I need to see this? I traced the edges of the curling parchment with one hand, using the other to play with my braid as I scanned the page. I stopped only to suck in a breath so sharp it made me cough once I reached the section on symbols. "Vitalara! This has to be it, right?" I kept reading until another familiar word leapt out at me. "How could I have forgotten that the Thaloria Festival was held originally in her honor?" This had to be it, if anyone could give me a lead on where to start looking, it would be her. I didn't believe in coincidences, so with the timing of the festival and her connection to Thorne, I just *knew* she was my path forward.

The atmosphere instantly lightened, and I sensed a brief burst of pride that felt like Nivaire; goddess of ardor, beauty, and sensuality, who'd made it her mission to increase my confidence and had apparently been watching the show with reserved amusement. "Thank you. And you, Thorne." It was him, after all, who'd thought to direct me to his twin. He may have just found the answer to all my problems.

Chapter 5

"Father? Are you home?"

I knocked on the door, muscles relaxing some when it didn't swing open like before. Someone raised their voice inside, and I realized with a start that maybe I should come back another time. Mama's books weren't going anywhere.

The door slammed open, and Isolde gestured impatiently at me. "Come on, come in. It's good that you're here. You were my next stop." Her hair brushed along her shoulders as she marched back into the main room, and I didn't dare try to get the blonde strand I spotted stuck to the back of her favorite onyx tunic.

It was darker inside, the hearth needing more fuel, and from the kitchen drifted the faint scent of burned biscuits. The mess had only grown worse since my last visit. I fought a gulp and looked nervously at my father the second Isolde turned away. He widened his eyes and shook his head like there was nothing he could do. I began mouthing furiously at him to send her away, but she turned to face us right as I'd finished my third unsuccessful attempt, missing his slight shrug in response.

Isolde's voice cut through the silence like a sharp blade. "Why was Elise speaking to Alden? Why have you been acting so strange lately?"

The room was silent as I considered my response. My father was no help, and had fixed me with a pointed look while he waited for the answer to the first part of her question. I might have held strong in my conviction to not involve her, but when her fingers tightened around the handle of her cane and she grimaced down at it, I knew she was falling back into old insecurities that we assumed her incapable of helping. Too fragile to handle the truth.

Our father sensed the same, and sighed. "It's bad enough that Elise got the truth out of me. I'd hoped to spare you girls."

She demanded an answer once more. "What happened?"

This was going to take a while. I made my way to the kitchen, hoping they would follow me, and cracked one of the windows to rid the room of the lingering bitter smell. It looked like the biscuits had already been disposed of, at least. I'd inherited my father's baking skills, as in we both had none.

He took a seat at the head of the table and Isolde followed, taking the chair to his right. While I busied myself using his meager supplies to make us something edible to eat, our father explained to Isolde what he had told me.

Her frigid demeanor thawed in degrees as she realized just how bad things had gotten. She was definitely upset that he'd waited until it was almost too late to tell us, but her analytical mind was already busy working through possible solutions.

Never one to forget easily, my father turned his focus onto me. His gaze, typically warm and reassuring, now bore a hint of concern sprinkled with censure. "Now what's this about you speaking to Alden?"

That pulled Isolde from her thoughts. Her sharp eyes narrowed. "You went to the council, didn't you?"

"Yes." I shifted uncomfortably, feeling the weight of their attention pressing down on me. "They turned me down. But Alden..." I hesitated, sensing Isolde's impatience building like a gathering storm. "He made me an offer."

A tense silence hung in the air as I struggled to find the right words. "He'll forgive Father's debt if I can find him the vitalara plant within four weeks."

My sister gasped. Like Isa, Isolde had a basic knowledge of various plants and herbs, both arcane and not. A product of living with our mother. Whether my father knew just how impossible it would be to procure was another story. "Why would you accept such a bargain?"

"What choice did I have?" I shot back. "It was that or risk losing everything. At least now we have a chance, however slim it may be. That's why I'm here. I need to look for answers in Mama's books."

As much as I'd like to keep them all at the cottage with me, there simply wasn't enough room. Besides, they were a point of pride for my father. While the rest of the village had viewed her with distaste and wariness, he'd been filled with pride for her talented magic, and kept her books on display in the spare room.

"Like what?" Isolde asked.

I slid into the seat beside her and slumped forward on the table. "Thorne showed me that vitalara is one of Sylvane's symbols—the goddess of wheat and bountiful harvests—and that the Thaloria Festival used to be performed in her honor to symbolize the beginning of the growing season and the promise of abundance in the coming months."

"His twin, right?" my sister asked.

"You have a surprisingly good memory sometimes. Yes."

"Yeah, well, I guess you can't accuse me of listening with half an ear any more."

"Make it a pattern, then we'll see. So, if we want to request her assistance, we're going to first need to research how to best appeal to her. Even if she wants to respond, she's most likely too weak. Minor deities, especially when they've fallen out of popularity, always have trouble touching this realm. That's why we need to see if there's some way to use the festival to strengthen her, at least temporarily. People may have forgotten its roots, but that doesn't mean the impact isn't still felt. It's performed in her name, after all."

"And you can't just ask her like you would your others?"

"I've formed mutual working relationships with them that have taken years to develop. I don't know her or her communication style well enough to take that route, and that's if she's even able to respond and a trickster doesn't try in her stead. The others are still somewhat worshiped, if not widely, and so they're more powerful. Unlike Thorne, she hasn't responded in any manner to a summons, prayer, or plea in decades according to my research last night. It was only a footnote, but it's important to remember."

My father leaned back in his chair, crossing his arms over his chest in a familiar manner. "What *exactly* are you looking for? Maybe we can help."

"Information on a ritual or ceremony that might tell me how to best reach her. It's possible that she's gone somewhat dormant, and it will require a lot of power." My peers were surprisingly tolerant regarding my attendance at celebrations, but it was just fine with me that I would be missing it this year. Nothing was more important than this; everything rested on my success.

Isolde nodded. "Alright, go pick the best ones. Mama might not have taught me like she did you, but I still have a good idea of what you're looking for. We'll help."

I hovered in place for a moment, shocked into stillness until my father made a shooing motion with his hand. "Go on," he commanded.

I did as asked, returning with the four or five tomes that were most likely to contain the information I needed and setting them gently in the center of the table. Together, we sifted through the yellowed pages of the old books my mother had collected over the years.

The musty scent of old paper hung heavy in the air, mingling with the faint aroma of dried herbs and lingering traces of long-extinguished incense. The soft rustle of pages turning filled the room, punctuated by the occasional creak of the wooden floorboards beneath our feet as we shifted in our seats.

As the day waned, the dim light filtering through the cracked window softened. Occasional murmurs echoed off the walls, hesitant pronunciations of unrecognized words punctuated by excited whispers whenever someone found something of interest.

It was just when the ache behind my eyes grew unbearable that Isolde exclaimed, "Found it!"

I hastily pushed my chair back and struggled to avoid colliding with the table as I navigated around it with tired and stiff limbs to reach her side. Isolde gestured toward the passage she had uncovered, blue eyes sparkling. The worn pages of the book crackled softly beneath my fingertips as I leaned in to read, my breath catching as I scanned the faded text.

Words like "veil" and "offering" leaped out at me, sending shivers down my spine. The next line referred to invocation, and my pulse quickened with excitement. "This looks promising," I breathed. "It'll take me days to gather the rest of these supplies. Most likely right up until the day of the festival." Dragon's tears, and sandalwood... I already have a lot of these. Silver-thistle oil might be a tough find, but I have an abundance of quartz.

My father's voice brought me back to the present, his words laced with warmth. "If you need anything, Elise, please don't hesitate to ask. There are no words for how grateful I am to have such wonderful girls, willing to help me with this."

He pulled me into a tight hug, and my voice was muffled as I spoke into his shoulder. "Of course, Papa. We love you."

Isolde's attention wavered for a moment, her gaze flicking toward us before returning to the book before her. I leaned back to give her arm a quick, reassuring squeeze—the most she would accept—then sighed when she tugged affectionately at my streak of white hair, something Mama had done daily for years.

Chapter 6

THE NEXT WEEK PASSED in a blur. I'd just barely managed to find the penultimate ingredient I needed, as silver-thistle oil was hard to procure in this area and I'd used the last of my reserves several months ago. Preparations for the festival were well underway, and if Isa hadn't stopped by to drag me into the village, I might not have seen them this year at all. It was for the best, as I needed frankincense from the apothecary.

The sun had just dipped below the horizon, casting a golden glow over the village, and the cobblestone streets were bustling with a flurry of activity. The arcane lanterns were adorned with delicate ivy and small bouquets of wildflowers, their soft glow casting dancing patterns on worn stones below. Garlanded archways spanned the thoroughfares, woven with vines and blooms in hues of green and silver. I wonder if anyone knew who those colors were really for, that the ivy symbolized growth and renewal, while the wildflowers represented rebirth and abundance. All symbols of Sylvane. Even the arrangement of the garlands followed a carefully crafted pattern, designed to invoke the blessings of the goddess and ensure a bountiful harvest in the coming season; things we'd done for so long that we all knew it had to be arranged "just so" but with no thought as to why.

Along the main square, villagers chatted as they set up stalls filled with offerings of freshly harvested fruits, colorful flowers, and handcrafted trinkets. Children darted between the merchants, their laughter echoing through the air as they chased after fireflies.

Callista wrenched her hand from mine with a squeal, running into the crowd as a friend called her name. I looked at Isa, but she just shrugged. "It's alright. Callum, would you like to join them?"

He nodded eagerly, following after his sister at a much more sedate pace. Seconds later, they were gone from view.

"So," she said, turning to me. "Where to first?"

Her dark-blonde hair was fairly tamed for once, tied back in a neatly done braid that fell midway down her back. The dark circles under her eyes that had finally managed to disappear several months ago were back with a vengeance, only working to highlight the cornflower-blue of her irises. I knew she wasn't getting out enough either, because the freckles sprinkled across her soft cheeks were half the number they were last year, and lighter too.

Maybe once I fixed things, she wouldn't be as stressed. I knew it was hard for her to have Finn gone all the time.

"I'm stopping at the apothecary first. Are you coming?"

"Well, I can't imagine it will take very long. I have the entire afternoon to help set up; you're the one short on time."

I winced at the reminder, fiddling nervously with the ends of my hair as we walked, the locket a comforting weight against my chest. Telling her everything had been difficult, but the rest of us agreed that it wasn't fair to leave her out of it. The betrayal of not being involved in our attempt to fix things might've overshadowed our good intentions, and that was the last thing we wanted. She'd felt guilty, of course, and wished she'd been the one to make the deal with Alden in the first place. No one could refute that Callum's health was the most important thing, but she still felt responsible. It had taken hours to try to convince her otherwise.

It was only a short walk before we approached the quaint storefront. The apothecary was one of the few places in the village where my presence wasn't just tolerated, but welcomed, so I ended up spending more time there than any other establishment.

Isa gave my hand a reassuring squeeze as we entered the shop. The bell above the door chimed softly, announcing our arrival. The interior was dimly lit, shelves lined with jars of dried herbs and small tins, and the air was heavy with the scents of lavender and mint. I grew most of my own herbs, but some I preferred to buy already prepared for storage.

Ms. Wilder looked up from her work behind the counter, eyes crinkling warmly. "Well, if it isn't Elise and Isa! What can I do for you two today?"

I returned her smile, even though it took effort. She reminded me so much of my mother that sometimes it hurt to speak with her. I saw the older woman she would have become if her illness hadn't stolen her from us. "We're just here to pick up some frankincense," I explained.

She nodded, setting aside her project to shuffle over to the shelf behind her, then selected a small vial. "Here you go, dear. We just got a new batch the other week. Is there anything else? Not out of valerian yet?"

I shook my head, tucking the vial into the satchel slung over my shoulder. "No, thank you. This will do just fine."

Sometimes an entire hour would pass while I perused all the new arrivals to the shop and played with Grumpy, her calico cat that was the opposite of her namesake and sometimes ventured out from the back to greet customers, so it was strange to be so brief today. After a bit more idle catching up, I paid her then left, once more entering the chaotic square.

Isa bid me farewell with a tight hug, her head only reaching my shoulder as she whispered a few words of encouragement before she left. I watched her disappear into the crowd, a brief pang of loneliness tugging at my heart as everyone instinctively shifted to give me a wide berth.

The fromagerie sat several storefronts back, and I briefly considered stopping by to say hello to Esme. When I noticed her bickering quietly with her father and stretching her arms out in front of her, though, I realized it would probably be an unwelcome distraction. Judging by the steadily increasing volume of their argument, she'd have a lot to tell me next time we spoke.

Turning back toward the wide-open expanse behind the last row of buildings, I took a moment to breathe in the smoke from a nearby fire before starting the long journey back. The shadows had grown long and the air brisk by the time I threw the door open to the cottage. I slipped off my shoes with a sigh of relief, relishing the sensation of the cool floorboards beneath my feet as I padded across the room. The weight of my responsibilities pressed down on me like a leaden cloak.

I couldn't fail.

To lose the home we'd grown up in, the land we'd cultivated, the belongings my father held near and dear, the trinkets my mother had gathered over the years all to pay a greedy and unconscionable man... It was infuriating.

I paused to light a few candles, their gentle glow casting elongated shadows against the cream-colored walls. The soft crackle of flames filled the silence, a familiar sound that I tried to let calm me. I was lucky to have learned how to ward a hearth early on in life so that the fire couldn't escape. In my childhood home and now my own, the fire ran regardless of whether we were home or not.

Silas greeted me with a soft *mew* from his perch on the windowsill, his golden eyes gleaming in the dim light as he jumped down. He brushed against my legs, his purr echoing throughout the room. I scooped him up into my arms, his warmth and weight a comforting presence against my front. He made a quiet noise when I kissed the top of his head, snuggling in to rest his chin on my arm.

With Silas settled in my arms, I made my way to the stone hearth, where a pot of stew I'd prepared earlier in the day simmered over the dying flames. The aroma of savory herbs and root vegetables wafted through the air, stirring memories of simpler times spent with my family when I was younger and we ate every meal together.

Sinking into the worn armchair and absorbing some of the room's warmth before I ate, I let out a weary sigh, my thoughts drifting back to the day's events. I had everything I needed, but would it work? In just a few short hours, I would be performing the ritual, yet after a week of preparation I still somehow didn't feel ready. Just one narrow window, and then the best lead we had would be gone, and we'd need to start from scratch.

It was times like this where I felt my loneliness acutely. If I didn't have Silas... He rubbed his head against my arm, and I clucked my tongue. "I know," I murmured, resting my head against the back of the chair. "It'll be alright."

I KNELT BEFORE THE base of the giant oak tree, tucking stray pieces of hair behind my ears, and shuddered, fingers digging painfully into the soil. A week of working nonstop to make sure everything was just right, a week of holding my emotions in and staying strong for my father so that he didn't worry, all while bearing the weight of being his only solution. Maybe he was resigned to the inevitable, but I wasn't. Not one bit.

Now that I was finally at the moment I'd been working toward for days, I couldn't hold back the emotions. My vision grew blurry, the trees around me becoming amorphous blobs. I sniffled and wiped my hands off on my dress, using my wrists to rub my eyes with a gentle chastisement. *That's enough. You have work to do.*

The distant sound of the festival filtered through the trees, the music and excited shouts signaling that the celebration had reached its zenith, which also meant that the veil was finally at its thinnest. Above, the full moon cast a bright glow on the clearing, illuminating the space I had chosen for the ritual. I could think of no better place than the forest right outside the cottage. I was deeper in than usual, as it had been difficult to find the perfect spot, but I knew it once I saw it.

I lit my white candle and took a moment to run my fingers over the symbols, words, and protection sigils carved into its surface before setting it aside and moving on to the next step. The air was thick with the scent of frankincense, rosemary, and lavender as I purified the area and my tools with the mixture I'd created earlier, the smoke swirling around me in a comforting embrace.

With trembling hands, I focused on my intentions while I inscribed my message onto a small piece of parchment, then rolled it tightly and placed it at the base of the tree. Pulling the stopper from the miniature bottle I'd brought, I then carefully dropped a generous amount of silver-thistle oil infused with sandalwood, quartz, rose petals, and other ingredients onto the parchment.

Next, I made my offering of freshly picked starflowers—the tiny, star-shaped blooms produced a calming fragrance that went a long way toward clearing my head—and a decent pour of sweet mead. As I settled into quiet meditation, I focused my mind on my message, visualizing it transcending the realms to reach her.

To invite the gods into the inner workings of your life would be to introduce probable chaos and ruin. They had no inclination toward subtlety, and the awful truth was that they were often bored and mischievous due to the nature of their immortality. Though some, like Thorne, were widely known for their innate touch of cruelty and indifference. Ironic, considering he was also the god of justice and punisher of broken oaths.

Before so many of them had retreated into the stars for their long rest, making way for their more popular counterparts, they'd walked the earth for centuries, worshiped and reviled in equal measure. While I often consulted my deities for spell work and insight, it was a new experience to make a request of this magnitude. So many things were necessary for this to work. *If* she even heard me, *if* she decided to offer us aid, if she even *could* help. Just because the vitalara plant was one of her symbols, didn't mean she magically had all the answers.

Once I was satisfied, many minutes later, I whispered an invocation, the words echoing through the stillness of the night. The sounds of celebration had long since faded, leaving just the rustle of leaves and the distant *hoot* of an owl. All that was left was to ignite the parchment and watch as flames consumed it until only ashes remained. It wasn't like I expected a sign right away, but I still felt the barest brush of disappointment when nothing happened.

"A waiting game," I muttered to myself, taking my hair out of its tight braid and brushing it as best I could with my fingers so that it hit my back in loose waves. It was still slightly damp from being washed earlier, and I hoped the cool night air would dry it quickly. I leaned my back against the tree, telling myself I deserved a minute to relax. *I'll just close my eyes for a minute.*

Chapter 7

SOMETHING SNAPPED, BRINGING ME to full alertness within seconds. I woke with a crick in my neck and groaned softly when I arched my back to rid it of its stiffness. One bleary blink of my eyes revealed a dark sky overhead. I took a deep breath in, eyes falling shut once more at the soothing scent of the loamy soil beneath me and the fresh dew coating the grass. It wasn't the first night I'd fallen asleep outside after a ritual, and it likely wouldn't be the last.

Rubbing my eyes, I glanced around, but could only see dark treelike shapes as my eyes hadn't adjusted yet. I sat up straight, propping my back up against the tree, expecting to see a deer wander into sight any second. After several minutes of waiting, I resigned myself to the fact that I was alone. Whatever had woken me was long gone. I rose to my feet and extinguished the candle that had burnt itself down to a nub, stretching my arms over my head and getting the blood flowing to my legs so I didn't collapse the second I tried to take a step.

As I gathered my things, I looked over the offerings I'd left and noticed that one of the starflowers seemed to be missing. The thought of some little creature running off with it held between its jaws made me smile to myself as I brushed the dirt off my dress and began the short walk back home. Something told me Sylvane wouldn't begrudge whatever had run off with it.

It must have been later than I realized, as the sky was just beginning to lighten when I reached the cottage, the horizon painted a light-gray hue that signaled the coming dawn. Each step felt heavier than the last, my muscles protesting the short rest spent on the hard ground. I rubbed at my lower back in small circles, promising myself I wouldn't do it again anytime soon and resolved to make a pot of green tea with chamomile as soon as I got back.

I didn't bother dancing from stone to stone like usual on the large stepping stones that lined the path to my cottage, instead walking sedately on the grass in between them. When I reached my cottage, I threw open the door, wasting no time in stripping out of my damp clothes and into a warm, light-pink sleep gown that hugged my frame loosely and fell to just below my knees. I sat at the dresser my father had carved by hand, running a hand over all the keepsakes I'd accumulated over the years until I reached my hairbrush. A small, glazed vase with fresh wildflowers sat to my right, the scent doing wonders for my aching head.

With a tired sigh, I ran the brush through my tangled hair, stopping to pull out the occasional twig. The familiar routine brought a feeling of normalcy that I'd been sorely lacking over the past week. Sleep was calling to me, my bedroom cozy and warm. The walls were painted a soft shade of lavender, deepened by the light from the hearth and the gray lightening sky outside the window. A rustic wooden bedframe sat in the center of my room, painted with vines and butterflies from when Callista had wanted more practice before painting some of the items my father had crafted. She was incredibly talented for her age.

I gazed longingly at the patchwork quilt on my bed behind me, all done in shades of blue and cream, but knew I couldn't sleep yet. I still needed to hydrate, and then check on Silas.

Speaking of, the second I finished brushing my hair, Silas made himself known with a loud trill. I left my room, following his persistent meows as I walked from room to room, but not seeing him.

"Silas?" I headed into the kitchen, listening as his caterwauls increased in volume. "I'm here, Silas. That's enough yowling. Are you hungry?"

I picked up my mortar to begin grinding the herbs for my tea when I realized he'd stopped making noise altogether. Somehow, his sudden silence in response to my question was more concerning than the nonstop communication from moments before.

It wasn't until I turned around that I realized why.

The sound of my mortar crashing to the wooden floorboards shattered the tense atmosphere, as I noticed that there, seated at my kitchen table, was a woman. My heart pounded with a mixture of fear and curiosity as I stared at the mysterious intruder before me, barely holding back a startled shriek.

I scanned her features in seconds, and quickly realized I was looking at one of the most stunning beings I'd ever seen. Recognition hit me so quickly that it left me reeling. And yet, what caught my attention most was the starflower adorning her hair, the very same one that had been missing earlier in the forest.

"You're here," I whispered.

"You needed me," she stated plainly. Like it was a given, and not a monumental amount of effort on her part. "I've been dormant for so very long," she said with a sigh. "And then you called."

The morning light that streamed through the kitchen window graced her, casting a delicate halo around her figure. Pointed ears were barely visible from beneath the cascade of long, dark-silver hair that formed loose curls at the ends, and hooded eyes looked out at me behind long, pitch-black lashes. She had no pupils, just solid irises that were a soft gold hue, yet I knew she was examining me in the same manner. I suddenly felt lacking in comparison, standing there in just my sheer nightgown. It was *not* a garment designed for greeting company.

I crossed my arms over my chest. "I don't understand. How are you here? And why? Why come? I mean... N-not that I'm questioning you or..." I trailed off, well aware that my cheeks were turning pink as I grew more and more flustered.

Her laugh was low and quiet. "I'm here to help," she declared. "As requested."

"I didn't mean for you to come here! I didn't even think that was possible."

The shadow of uncertainty that crossed her face seemed out of place and made me wish I could snatch my words back. "I'm sorry, I didn't mean to sound ungrateful. I just... This doesn't *happen*."

Sylvane nodded from where she sat at my kitchen table and leaned forward, watching me with an almost affectionate look. "You did everything perfectly. The veil, the ritual, the festival... Did you know it was observed across the country yesterday? That's countless of people celebrating in my name. Could I have found some other way to answer your request? I'm sure. But when I realized how easy it was to descend... How could I resist?"

"How indeed," I muttered.

She arched one perfectly groomed dark brow, and I felt my face flush once more. "You must be tired. I will feed Silas, and you should get some sleep. We can speak when you wake."

Silas meowed in agreement, but I was a bit more hesitant. Leave this... this *goddess* to her own devices in my humble cottage? What if she thought it wasn't clean enough? Or too cluttered? Or worse,

I woke up and found she'd disappeared without a trace. "Maybe we should find you somewhere nicer to stay…"

She rose from the chair in one smooth movement, revealing a tall, willowy silhouette. I had to crane my neck back to watch her as she approached, as I only came up to her bust. "I like it here. Cozy and warm, with magic embedded in the walls. Besides, who would take me in? The inn is likely full of visitors from last night's celebration." Sylvane raised one long-fingered hand, and the dying basil on my windowsill perked up immediately, leaves straining toward the window as they grew unnaturally fast. I gaped at her, taken aback by her little smirk. "Mutually beneficial. See? Now go rest."

SYLVANE WAS RIGHT—I HAD needed to rest. I felt much more in control of myself when facing her a second time. I'd wandered out of my room after spending an embarrassing amount of time trying to tame my hair into something presentable before giving up, leaving it draped loose around my shoulders. I found her on the settee near the hearth with Silas purring away on her lap. The position of the sun outside told me that it was around noon, which meant I'd been sleeping for hours.

"Are you hungry?"

Even if I was, I didn't think I could stop looking at her long enough to eat. Besides, I wanted answers more than anything else.

"I've left you offerings sometimes," I told her.

"Yes. You have. Why is that?"

I shrugged, feeling strangely on display. "Seemed only fair. Why honor one twin only to ignore the other? You're part and parcel, of sorts. Although I never felt you like I did the others. Like I did Thorne."

She frowned before returning to her impassive state. "Yes, well. Eternity is a long time, and dormancy is a necessary part of the cycle. I was aware, just... conserving energy. My followers have greatly decreased over the years, but that doesn't mean I am left with none."

"So you chose now... me... to help? To wake?"

She hiked one delicate shoulder up in a bare shrug, her loose dress slipping down to expose some of her pale skin. It was made of a texture we didn't see much of around here—slinky and soft—and colored a pale-blue shade that almost seemed to shimmer when the sun hit it. I looked away, rubbing my thumb over my locket, and took a seat in the armchair across from her.

"I'd like to help you," she finally said.

"You mean help me physically find the vitalara plant?"

"Yes."

That was it. No elaboration, no reasoning. Just that she wanted to help me. That she had come down to live amongst mortals for up to *three weeks* with no explanation simply because my line honored her brother?

What else was I to do other than graciously accept her help?

"Okay. I suppose it's settled. I'm going to freshen up, and then make something for us to eat." I paused at that, stopping mid-movement as I stood from the chair. "You do eat, right?"

She laughed. "Yes. I eat. In fact, I can help. In exchange for letting me stay here and impose on you, I can cook our meals."

"Impose on me?" I exclaimed. "It's an honor just to have you here. You don't need to earn your keep. It's enough that you'd lend me your knowledge and assistance when the most I was expecting was a cryptic message sent through a dream, if anything."

Her expression briefly darkened. "Not an honor, just a kindness. An adventure. Don't be afraid to bring things to my attention, no matter how small."

Was she used to mortals carving their lives out around her wants and needs and was worried I would follow suit? I thought about making a joke, but she was being entirely serious and deserved the same in response. "Understood. You could never be an imposition, but I'll keep it in mind regardless."

That seemed to be enough for her, as she gave me a small dip of her pointed chin then resumed massaging Silas's favorite spot behind his ears.

It took us around an hour to finally sit down. We ate in relative silence, a sweet concoction Sylvane had whipped up with the last of my golden honey and lavender bread, along with some fragrant herbs. Simple, but thoughtful.

"So," she said as she began to clear her side of the table. I watched her move over the rim of my still-steaming mug of tea as I took a small sip. Her silver hair slid along her shoulders and chest as she moved, cascading in waves down her back. I happened to know that it smelled faintly of wildflowers from when I'd squeezed past her earlier; the curse of living in such a small home. Somehow, I knew it would only get worse. I'd never lived with anyone other than my sisters for longer than several days, and that was just from Esme staying the occasional weekend. I knew with sudden clarity that it would be the trial Sylvane warned me it might be, but not for the reasons she'd assumed.

"So," I replied, pushing my chair back to get started on my own mess.

The sun caught her eyes as she turned, highlighting their otherness. She stopped me with just a look, waiting until I sat back down to continue happily working. "Your tea is still warm. Drink up while I take care of things."

It felt... wrong... to have a goddess clear my plates. But she seemed to enjoy the task, humming a melodic tune I'd never heard before under her breath as she worked. I did as asked, settling back into my chair and clasping the blue earthenware mug between my palms, content to keep watching her flit around the kitchen. Unlike me, she was able to reach the top shelves of my open cabinets with ease as she put things away.

She joined me at the table once finished, observing me avidly as I finished my drink. "You have questions for me," she stated.

"Yes, I... Yes. As I said the other night, I made a deal with someone that I would find him the vitalara plant within four weeks in exchange for forgiving my father's debt. He loaned him the coin he needed to purchase medicine for my sick nephew, and then the amount spiraled from there."

"Despicable."

"I rather think so. The only thing I know about the plant is its properties, that it's rare and rumored to be extinct, and meticulous to prepare. I've searched all my books, but any information listed is incredibly sparse."

Sylvane nodded, sweeping her hair back from her face and crossing her thin yet defined arms on the scarred tabletop as she leaned forward. Her form was so lithe, giving the impression that she possessed the fragility of a mortal, but I already knew from watching her move that her strength far surpassed mine. "I know that much."

"The only thing I managed to find was that it's included in your list of symbols. I thought..."

"You thought that meant I would know more about where to find it?"

"Yes."

Her sigh was deep. "I'm afraid that I don't have all the answers you seek. It *is* rare, and it only grows on Earth, not in my realm.

It has incredible medicinal properties, and works wonders for spell work given its arcane nature. Most everyone could find some use from it, but it is best known for warding off disease and infection. In the past, it could be found at the base of my temples, where it was grown in offering to me. It also thrived in sacred groves, where the veil between the mortal realm and the divine was thinnest. It isn't the kind of plant you would find in the wild; it has to be cultivated with precise care."

"Where is the nearest one of either?"

"The only groves left are overseas, but my nearest temple... I believe there is one in Elmspring. The next would be over a month's travel from here."

I absorbed this information, my mind racing with possibilities. Elmspring was only a day away if the weather was good. In fact, we did a fair amount of trading with them. "We could check there," I suggested, my heart pounding with excitement. "If the vitalara once grew at the base of your temples, perhaps there are still remnants of it to be found."

Sylvane's hesitation gave me pause. She worried her plush bottom lip with a pointed canine as she watched me, and I stayed silent in the hopes that she might speak her mind. "I have been gone for some time," she finally said.

"Yes?"

"And so my followers have greatly decreased in number. It stands to reason that my temples would have as well."

I hadn't even considered that. Despite her warning, I couldn't help the sudden surge of determination. We finally had a lead! All we could do was check, then reassess if we didn't find anything. "I've never left the village, but we trade with Elmspring regularly. I can go into the village tomorrow and see about accompanying a merchant on their next trip, if it's soon enough." I twisted a lock of my hair around my finger, muttering the next part. "That's if they even agree."

"Why would they not?"

"Witches aren't very popular here. I can't think of a member of this village who would willingly let me accompany them for a long journey in an enclosed space."

"They will," Sylvane declared. "I will be with you." I hated to think that her opinion of me might sour when she saw how they reacted to me. All I could do was nod, hoping that the experience wouldn't be too humiliating. And it wasn't like there weren't other ways to get to Elmspring. Granted, they would take longer, but it would all be worth it if we found the vitalara.

With renewed resolve, I rose from the table, my mind already turning to preparations for the journey that awaited us.

Chapter 8

THE RUMORS BEGAN THE second we stepped foot in the village the next day. People hurried past, their faces a mixture of curiosity and suspicion as they stole glances at us while we moved through the crowd. I'd known we would be a spectacle, but the reality of it was so much more difficult than I'd anticipated. It was more attention than I had ever received in my lifetime.

The villagers whispered among themselves, their words carried on the breeze in the crisp morning air. "Who's with the witch?"

someone murmured, their voice hushed with awe and disbelief. "Look at her *eyes*."

Words like "deity" and "goddess" were thrown around, which was unsurprising. We might be a fairly isolated place, but we were no strangers to the deities who walked amongst mortals on occasion.

Sylvane moved with an effortless grace, commanding attention partly just by the way she stood a full head taller than anyone around her. Her attire was simple yet elegant, a light-pink gown that came to my ankles when I wore it but only hit her mid-calf. Long hair cascaded down her back in a waterfall of shimmering, silvery waves, catching the light in a mesmerizing display. She preferred to wear it loose or in a quick braid, she'd told me that morning. According to her, patience was something she was short on, and that included for doing her hair. I wasn't sure I'd agree, given her endless patience with me so far.

I kept my head low, hoping to avoid any confrontations. Meanwhile, Sylvane appeared calm and composed, completely unbothered by the attention. As we made our way deeper into the village, I couldn't shake the feeling of unease that settled in the pit of my stomach. I tugged nervously at my locket, trying to blend into the background as best I could, but I knew it was futile.

Her arm briefly brushed against mine. While I would have thought it a consequence of simply walking too close, her soft smile when I peeked up at her dispelled that notion. It was a small thing, yet I already felt more like I was standing on solid ground.

The village square bustled with activity. Merchants peddled their wares, people crowded the walking spaces, and livestock bleated in the distance. The air was filled with the scent of freshly baked bread and the earthy aroma of herbs and spices, mingling with the faint perfume of the flowers for sale.

One vendor stopped Sylvane with an enthusiastic wave, handing her a rose the color of her dress, his expression starstruck. She accepted it with a grin, bowing her head toward him in thanks before continuing on. Already, he turned to brag to the woman at the stall beside him that she'd accepted it.

The second we were out of view, she stopped to hand it to me. "I—but this is yours," I stammered.

She shrugged, her smile growing sly. "But it matches your blush so well." My cheeks ignited and, to avoid any further embarrassment, I tucked it into my breast pocket before hurrying along, ignoring the warm sound of her laughter as it rang out behind me.

As we approached our destination, a small tavern located in the very center of the village, my nerves worsened. The tavern keeper, a stout man with a jovial demeanor that I'd only seen from afar, greeted us with a welcoming smile as we entered.

"The witch! And a friend," he exclaimed, eyes widening in disbelief. "Word spread the second you entered the village, though I never expected this to be your stop. What a pleasant surprise. You can call me Garrick."

Pleasant? *Me*?

His excitement was palpable, infectious even, and I found myself smiling back in spite of my nerves. "We were hoping to speak with you about your trading schedule," I explained. "We're in need of transportation to Elmspring as soon as possible, if you happen to have any room."

If he wondered how I knew that he made frequent trips to Elmspring for supplies, he didn't ask. I'd never admit that I could listen to Isa or my father speak about the goings on here for *hours* before I called it a day.

His eyes lit up at the prospect. "Of course, of course," he declared. "It would be an honor to have such esteemed company. We'd leave in several days' time, possibly four from now."

Relief flooded through me at his words. *Finally* something was going our way. I thanked him profusely, feeling a weight lift off my chest as the realization sunk in that we were that much closer to possibly finding the vitalara. And if we left in several days, then we'd still have under two weeks left until Alden's deadline by the time we got back.

Sylvane nudged me gently once he'd turned away to help a customer, giving me a quick wink. "See?" she murmured. "It's all working out. You didn't even need me here."

I scoffed. "Don't think for a second that he'd invite me so enthusiastically if it weren't for you."

The corners of her mouth turned down. "You're likable, Elisette. And if the people here are too closed-minded to realize that just because you were born with magic, then they're missing out. Besides, part of being brave sometimes means giving people a chance to show you something different."

I shook my head, thankful when she didn't push things any further. It was embarrassing enough that she'd noticed.

"Come on," she whispered conspiratorially. "I miss Silas already."

Chapter 9

"ARE YOU SURE THIS fits me okay?" Sylvane asked, giving a twirl that made the hem of her skirt flare out. She'd ordered several outfits from the seamstress in the village, and had gone to pick them up today. That it had only taken a couple days was incredible, when I knew it typically took several weeks.

The dress she currently wore was of a style I didn't usually see in the village: a fitted bodice that hugged her slim waist nicely, long sleeves, and a skirt that swept the ground as she walked. Delicate embroidery lined the neckline, cuffs, and hem, shimmering from the iridescent thread that must have been a special request. It was a soft, pale green shade that she seemed to favor, and she'd finished the look with a loose belt just above her waist.

"It's beautiful on you."

She beamed, twirling once more, and I curled up in the armchair to continue watching her. Along with another gown, she'd also ordered several long, sweeping skirts, as well as a set of loose-fitting tunics and trousers. It was quite the collection.

"It matches your eyes, don't you think? A lovely, flattering color."

I clamped my mouth shut, pretending I hadn't heard her and not being very discreet about it if her laugh was any indication.

Outside I could hear the faint tread of someone walking up the path to my home, and sank further into my chair. Another thing that was different—the sheer amount of visitors. Now that the village was aware we had a goddess among us, *everyone* had come seeking healing of some sort. This morning, the blacksmith had dropped by for a splinter. A *splinter*. The *blacksmith*. Needless to say, he'd spent the entire time fixated on Sylvane as she'd moved about the cottage fetching whatever I'd needed, even though I had insisted that she take some time to rest.

"I've rested enough," she'd argued. "Let me be useful to you."

And so I did. Did I really need tea every several hours? Of course not. But the ecstatic look on her face when she'd realized it was time for a new batch and she'd get to try a new combination of herbs was irresistible.

A knock sounded at the door, and Sylvane immediately walked over to open it. I scooted forward, waiting for the next nosy person to push their way in with something that would heal itself within the day. Surprise hit me when I recognized the young woman who sold flowers near the square. Her bright blonde hair was in an intricate braid today, and she wore the kind of dress that was reserved for special occasions. She flounced past Sylvane, doing a slow spin as she absorbed the interior of the cottage. "Oh." She giggled. "I thought it would be bigger."

Ah. It was *that* kind of visit. "What do you need help with?" I asked resignedly.

"Just a headache. It's dreadful, you know, standing out in the sun all day with the cloying scent of flowers," she lamented. "It's like it never fully goes away, and I end up smelling so fresh all the time."

"Such a hardship, I'm sure. I might have something to help."

Sylvane, ever oblivious to the undertones of her visit, adopted an expression of concern. "Oh, please take a seat," she urged.

The woman gleefully followed her to the settee. When Sylvane turned to go into the kitchen, she protested, "Oh no, please don't go. I'd love for you to sit with me for a spell." Though she seemed hesitant, Sylvane dutifully perched at the edge. "It's so rare that anything exciting ever happens in this small place," she continued. "And to think, you picked the *witch, of all people,* to grace with your presence." Her laughter had a spiteful edge. "We'll have to get you out and about, make introductions."

I stood abruptly, startling Sylvane. "I'll go fetch that medicine." I could still hear her chattering on from the kitchen; they shared a door, after all. She had moved on to admiring Sylvane's unique eyes, claiming they were the exact shade of wild honeysuckle. Which was only mildly true, but sounded much more romantic than the yellow peonies they more closely resembled.

I returned with her tea just in time to see her reach out and try to stroke the exposed, pointed tip of Sylvane's ear, having moved much closer within the last several minutes. Before I could even utter a word, Sylvane stood and approached me. "I'll be preparing *your* tea," she said with a wink, bending down to press a light kiss to my cheek. "I'll leave you to entertain Freya." When she didn't immediately pull away, my cheeks flooded with heat, feeling so warm that I knew they'd turned scarlet.

Feeling as if she'd made her point, Sylvane pulled away, pausing in the doorway of the kitchen to face the girl. "Such pettiness is entirely unbecoming, for future reference. You're lucky that Elisette is so kind as to still give you her headache remedy, because we both know she will, no matter what you and everyone else might think of her."

I... I couldn't even think, gaze locked on the place she'd just been standing. Sounds echoed from the kitchen, and I stared helplessly in its direction.

"Well, that couldn't have been any clearer," Freya said, standing and brushing off the front of her skirt like her brief stay had somehow dirtied it. "I suppose I did approach that a tad strongly. I didn't lie about my health, so if the goddess was right and you still plan to send me on my way with a treatment, I would be eternally grateful."

It took me several long seconds to find the words. "Yes, well... Yes." I dropped the sachet into her cupped hands. "Peppermint, chamomile, and lavender tea with a dash of celestis bark." I didn't bother mentioning the magic I'd infused it with. She wouldn't be here if she were looking for an ordinary version that she could purchase pre-mixed at the apothecary. "Brew it like you would any other tea, and it should stop the ache in its tracks."

She openly watched me, thankfully without any hostility, then gave me a genuine nod. "Thank you."

She left swiftly after that, sachet in hand, leaving me to return to my armchair.

"She's gone?" Sylvane asked as she brought me my latest mug of tea. It smelled of... lemon balm and oranges.

"Yes," I murmured, carefully taking the cup from her and blowing on it to cool the steaming contents.

"Pity." It was said so dryly that I couldn't help but laugh, moving the tea away so as not to burn myself.

"You didn't have to put on such a display," I teased. "A simple no would have sufficed."

Sylvane's easy grin disappeared, and I wished I could take the words back. "No display, Elise. Nothing I do or say is for appearances when it comes to you."

I could only nod and wonder when she'd started shortening my name.

"Besides," she added, tucking a chunk of hair behind a pointed ear. "I have a feeling she won't be the last."

In that, we were in agreement.

Of all my recent visitors, I somehow hadn't considered that my family would be among them. An oversight that Isolde swiftly corrected. According to her, she'd been "elected" by my father and Isa to visit and see just what was happening before reporting back. Lucky her that she could go straight to the source for her answers unlike everyone else who was still left wondering.

I sat down with her in front of the hearth while Sylvane gave us a moment of privacy, spending some time with Silas in the spare room that she'd claimed for her own.

"Her *eyes*," Isolde said, her own open wide. "Her *ears*."

"I know, I know. So different."

"I always knew you would do great things, but this... this is beyond what I ever expected."

Unused to such casual praise, I pretended she hadn't spoken, wishing I had Silas beside me to keep my hands busy. Besides, it wasn't like I'd done anything special.

Knowing me far too well, she laughed. "Alright, I'll stop. Besides, it hurts me to be nice far more than it hurts you to hear it. Just know that we're all rooting for you. Now, tell me how things got here. You did the ritual as planned?"

I explained how Sylvane had just... appeared and insisted on helping me see things through, and our upcoming trip to Elmspring. Isolde listened with an incredulous expression, fairly silent for the most part. I was envious of her ability to sit and listen without fidgeting; gods knew I'd been playing with my hands throughout the entire explanation.

She studied me for a moment, and when she finally spoke, it wasn't to say anything I'd been expecting to hear.

"Elise, I've never seen you like this before—all starry-eyed over someone. You seem smitten, and you've only known her for a handful of days."

A jolt of panic ran through me, and I quickly glanced around to ensure Sylvane was still occupied in her room. "Isolde, please," I protested, though my blush only seemed to deepen at her teasing. "We just met!"

She laughed, a warm and genuine sound that I hadn't heard from her in far too long. "You're lucky Isa isn't here, because she wouldn't stop after one small observation. Fine!" She raised her hands defensively. "We'll pretend like you don't wear that dazed expression whenever you simply mention her name."

I dropped my face into my palms, hoping it would be back to normal by the time I looked up.

"It's alright, Elise. It's just surprising since this is the first time you've ever... shown interest in someone. Don't worry, I'll be here when you get back, ready to help with whatever comes next. And whether you find the plant in Elmspring or not, I'm proud of you."

"Thank you," I said, my voice muffled by my hands. "For everything."

She squeezed my knee reassuringly. "What are sisters for?"

Chapter 10

"I JUST MISS HER so much," I whispered through a choked sob, curling up at the base of the tree outside the cottage.

Mama had passed a year ago today, greeting death peacefully in her sleep after the illness had finally taken her, and I was lost without her guidance and company. No more greeting the seasons with feasts and dancing. No more singing during our spell work, her clear voice ringing out across the cottage whenever she visited. No more small gifts left at my door because she found something that she just had to give me, knowing it would be perfect for one of my deities.

The last witch in the village. By the stars above was it lonely.

I wept quietly for some time, startled to a stop when something landed gently on my face. I opened my eyes to pluck it off, finding a leaf and sniffling as I examined it. It was a vibrant orange color, the exact shade of Mama's favorite dress, and as large as my hand, morphing into a fiery red at the top and yellow at the base. Truly something.

"Thank you," I whispered, holding it close.

I'd dry it and frame it later that night, displaying it above the mantle where I could see it every day.

WE SET OUT FOR Elmspring several days later as planned, the wagon laden with supplies and provisions to trade. I watched the familiar sights of my village fade into the distance, anticipation building in the pit of my stomach as we ventured into the unknown.

The journey passed in a blur of rolling countryside and winding dirt roads, the rhythmic *clip-clop* of the horses' hooves lulling me into a tired trance as the sun began to rise. Sylvane and I sat side by side on the rough wooden benches, quietly trading stories until I grew too sleepy to continue, my head accidentally landing against her shoulder as I began to nod off. The third time I lifted it back up, she pressed a cool hand to my forehead, keeping me there. "Stay," she whispered.

I shivered, turning my face into the soft fabric of her tunic.

Hours passed that I spent in and out of sleep until the air grew charged as we neared Elmspring. My nerves must have been more obvious than I thought, because Sylvane paused her conversation with Garrick where he sat up front, and turned to me. "This is a new experience for you, yes?"

"Yes." My voice shook slightly as my body rocked back and forth from the bumpy ride.

"I think you'll be surprised at how different it is. The world is so big, Elise, and you have seen so little of it. Let people surprise you."

Something told me that I'd only realize what she meant after we arrived. She had a tendency to slip in the most cryptic of statements sometimes, and I found it oddly endearing.

I glanced in her direction, surprised to find her already watching me. "You have the most stunning hair," she murmured, reaching over to run a wavy strand through her delicate fingers. I suppressed a shudder, mildly shocked by the flutter in my stomach.

"It's just brown," I told her.

She laughed. "Where you see *just brown*, I see a tapestry of warmth, the same rich hue of polished chestnuts. And this white streak... so unique. I've always admired it on witches."

Sylvane liked to slip compliments and praise into the most mundane of conversations, and *I* liked to think I'd gotten better at controlling my blushes. Even so, I had to look away. Being in such close proximity to her for such a prolonged amount of time... the scent of wildflowers on her hair, the glow of her eyes as she watched me with a strange fascination, it was all so new. She'd shifted closer after I fell asleep, probably so I could rest more comfortably, and our arms brushed together with each sway of the wagon.

"Yes, well," I mumbled, knowing full well that she was straining to hear me over the sounds of the horses. "You're the stunning one."

She shook her head, letting the strand of my hair fall from her fingers with a tiny smile. "Comes with the territory, I suppose. I don't want to be known for beauty, though. I want to be remembered for my contributions. To be treated like a regular person and not a spectacle."

Maybe we had more in common than I'd thought.

Garrick chose then to announce that we were approaching the outskirts of Elmspring. The landscape gradually shifted from the quiet countryside to the buzzing activity of the town as its narrow cobblestone streets and colorful facades came into view. The air hummed with energy as we drew nearer, alive with the steady stream of townsfolk going about their business. With each passing moment, I felt excitement building within me, a strange mixture of fear and eagerness.

It wasn't long before we pulled to a stop and piled out of the wagon. I offered to help Garrick unload, but several men had already filed out of a nearby building to begin lifting items out of the back.

"Now then," he said, leveling us with a serious look as he pulled us aside and out of the way. His gray hair had curled over his forehead, hiding the deep grooves there from view. "Don't forget that we'll be departing tomorrow morning, as I have business in town to attend to today. So, be sure to show on time."

Sylvane nodded dutifully while my attention was already drifting to the many people that passed us. Their garments were much the same, but sprinkled in were the types of attire that I only saw when we had an influx of visitors to the village.

A statue of a god sat in a place of prominence near the center of the square, though I wasn't able to tell who. Unlike our village, in addition to their evenly spaced arcane lanterns, they had large, stone fountains that used magic to keep the water moving. I could smell it in the air, the tang of ozone that came from large quantities of magic.

I didn't even realize Garrick had left until Sylvane's hand landed on my arm, making my entire body freeze. I could feel each individual fingertip, the heat radiating off her skin. She pulled away when I shuddered, politely pretending not to notice, hands landing on her hips as she examined our surroundings.

Bustling streets echoed with shouts and the clatter of carts. Sylvane's presence drew curious glances, her otherworldly beauty a shock, but no one appeared to be hostile or tried to approach us.

As we wandered through the lively marketplace, my jaw dropped at the sight of stalls adorned with mystical symbols and tables brimming with enchanted trinkets. It was a sight that both fascinated and unsettled me, stirring up emotions that I didn't have the time to pick apart. How could my mother have kept this hidden from me? It was one thing to know the world was bigger than our small village, but another to actually *see* it, and know that it was only a day's worth of travel away.

Venturing farther, we stumbled upon a quaint shop bearing runes on the doorframe. I hesitated at the threshold, unsure of what to expect, before a light, encouraging touch at my back had me pulling open the door.

Inside, the shopkeeper greeted us with a curious smile, her dark eyes alight with surprise as she took in Sylvane's distinctive appearance. She wore her fiery red hair in a style I'd never seen, piled atop her head in a complex, twisted style where several stray pieces trailed down her back. "Welcome," she said, her voice warm and inviting. Her words were laced with a hint of a lilting accent that I couldn't even hope to place. "What brings you to Elmspring?"

I cleared my throat. Tact had abandoned me, so I asked as straightforwardly as possible. "You wouldn't happen to have heard anything about the vitalara plant?"

She shook her head slowly. "Haven't heard that name in years. You would have to travel far to find it. That is, if it hasn't gone entirely extinct."

"Ah. Of course. In that case, we're seeking directions to Sylvane's temple, if you know the way." I didn't presume to think that all witches just *knew* the locations of the temples or shrines around them, especially in a town this big with so many shared deities as its patrons. But something told me she knew exactly where we needed to go.

The older woman cast another curious glance toward Sylvane, where she stood off to the side inspecting a display of shimmering aetheric quartz. "Her temple, you say? Why, it's been ages since anyone's shown interest in it. Although yes, I can help you."

My heart sank at her words, disappointment washing over me in a wave, but Sylvane remained composed, her expression betraying nothing. I listened carefully to the woman's instructions, thanking her profusely as we stepped back into the busy streets of Elmspring, but not before purchasing a miniature ceramic black cat that resembled Silas too much to pass up.

"THIS... CAN'T BE IT," I muttered, looking up at the weathered temple where it sat wrapped in vegetation. The afternoon sun had just begun its descent, casting a warm, golden hue over the landscape. The air was heavy with the scent of earth and moss, mingling with the sweet fragrance of the wildflowers that peeked through cracks in the crumbling stone walls. A gentle breeze carried with it the distant murmur of a nearby stream, but I could barely hear it over the rushing of blood in my ears.

This wasn't at all what I'd been expecting. I'd known better than to get my hopes up; Sylvane had warned me after all, and Isolde had reinforced it, but... I had.

Vines and ivy had crept up the cracked walls and claimed them for their own, making it clear that the temple had been abandoned for some time. Despite its neglected state, there was a certain beauty in its decay, a reminder of the resilience of nature. Fitting for the goddess of abundance and nurturer of fertile earth.

I peeked at Sylvane out of the corner of my eye, wondering how she felt.

She sensed my shifting attention and sighed. "This is just the way of things. I'm not upset, because it's how the cycle goes. No one is worshiped forever, no structure will stand forever."

We hiked through the undergrowth to the base of the building, examining the roughly shaped plots that clearly used to belong to an herb garden. Nothing remained but thorns and weeds. She didn't have to confirm it for me; the disappointed curve of her mouth did all the talking.

I dropped into the grass right where I stood, barely feeling the impact. My brain was working overtime, trying to find a positive outlook on the situation or conjure even a single next step that we could take. My father was going to lose his house, his land, his belongings, all because I'd *failed*—

Sylvane dropped down beside me, leaning in close like she wanted to touch me but wasn't sure if she was allowed to. I didn't want her to be a deity in that moment, I just wanted her to be *there*. I kept expecting to look at her and see... well, a goddess. And she was, that much was clear, but I also just saw Sylvane, who liked to sit in front of the hearth when it was first lit and spoiled Silas like nobody else, who had a near constant craving for strawberry jam and chamomile tea.

I threw myself into her arms without a second thought, exhaling for the first time in what felt like forever as her arms came up to circle my back, one hand landing on the back of my head to press my face into the curve of her neck. The dying light caught her hair, infusing it with a silver glow as it draped over her shoulder and brushed against my arm, thick with the scent of flowers.

It was like she'd sapped all my worries and brewing panic with just her touch, leaving behind a warm sensation. I'd never calmed so quickly before, and while I didn't think it would become a pattern, I would cherish it while it lasted. Nothing had ever felt so right.

I hadn't even known it was possible to feel this way for someone, despite seeing it in practice all around me my entire life. Though that path quickly led to thoughts of her leaving once our deadline was up, which was the exact opposite of what I needed to be thinking about at the moment.

I stirred in her embrace, biting my lip when her nose traced along my neck. Leaning back so I could observe her face, I brushed my fingers along the smooth skin of her cheek, lips ticking upward when she tilted her head ever so slightly into my caress.

"Thank you for being here," I whispered.

"I have cared for you longer than you even know," she said with a sigh, pressing a kiss to my palm where it lingered beside her mouth. "I wouldn't have responded to just anyone's plea with my presence."

My heart stopped. "I don't understand what you mean?"

"You were the first of your line to leave me offerings alongside Thorne in decades. I may have been dormant, but I was not oblivious to your existence. Your presence felt like—*feels* like—I never left."

"I never knew you could sense me."

"That makes it even more special that you did it for nothing in return. You're a kind person, Elise, and I wish everyone could see you just as I do. Besides, I was able to reach you occasionally. I sent you rats when your mother passed," she said softly.

Making a small, horrified noise, I held back an instinctive shudder. "That was you?! I figured I was doomed to bad luck forever, finding them under my bed and tucked away in the cabinets until the end of time." Now that I thought about it, I could remember seeing them under her list of animals associated with her.

"You didn't like them?" Her tone didn't change, but I could sense the barest note of vulnerability in the question. "They're such loyal and intelligent creatures. Amazing company."

"Oh, no! No, it was a very kind gesture," I rushed to assure her. Anything to stop that tiny frown from deepening.

The corner of her mouth tugged upward as she extended her hand into the tangle of grass beside us. I flew back, biting my lip against a shriek when, only seconds later, a gray rat crawled onto her hand.

"No fear," she whispered, rubbing its head with her long, slender fingers. "Look how friendly."

I scooted closer, peering over her arm to watch it twitch its little pink nose. I supposed it didn't seem so scary sitting in her palm like that, all sleek fur and big, dark eyes. Or maybe it was just that I knew she'd keep me safe from the big, bad rodent.

It made a quiet chirping noise that, despite my initial reaction, tugged at my heartstrings. "I suppose it's sort of cute," I acquiesced.

Sylvane sent a beaming smile my way that stole the breath from my next words, and a grin rose unbidden in response to her joy. She petted it several more times, then lowered her hand back to the grass so that it could go back into hiding.

"Were you... lonely? While you were sleeping?"

Her smile was almost sad. "Not how you would think of it. I wasn't tied to my physical form. I was aware but... not. Just a concept."

The thought of her going back to that horrified me, though I tried not to portray just how much. "But you like it here. Right?"

"I do." Just when I was about to ask more questions, she stretched, a low groan leaving her mouth that I knew without a doubt I'd like to hear again. "Now come," she said, climbing to her feet and holding a hand out for me to take. It was getting darker out, the air developing a bite to it. "Would you like to see the inside?"

"I... Yes. I would."

She walked to the bottom of the steps and raised a hand. Within seconds, the vines that traversed the entryway slid back to reveal a small path for us to walk through.

My jaw dropped.

"I may not be anywhere near as strong as I once was, but I am still capable of little things," she explained. A sense of solemnity washed over me as I followed her into the neglected shrine. The interior was a testament to the passage of time, with cobwebs draped from the parts of the ceiling that remained and the musty scent of decay permeating the space.

While her attention was captured by the other vine-covered doorways, I took a moment to pull a coin from my pocket and silently lay it upon her cracked altar, brushing aside some of the dust to make space for it.

Among the debris, I found remnants of faded, tattered tapestries depicting scenes of worship and intricately carved statues, their features weathered and eroded. My eyes were drawn to one particular scene, depicting a figure with stag horns that held a scythe, their form unrecognizable and yet not. "That's you?" I asked, already certain of the answer.

Sylvane approached, her gaze lingering on the cloth for a moment before she spoke. "That is one of my other forms," she explained quietly. "In ages past, I had the ability to take many shapes, to walk among mortals in various guises. But those days are long gone."

I let my hand brush against hers as we stared at the image, hoping to bring her some sort of solace, our pinkies briefly tangling. My heart pounded so loudly, it felt like it could be heard all the way from outside.

"It seems futile to search for the vitalara elsewhere," I murmured. "Even if we were to find another temple, the plant has likely been overharvested or died after being untended."

She made a thoughtful noise in agreement. "We're not giving up. We'll go back home tomorrow and make sure we've exhausted every approach."

My heart, having just begun to slow from our earlier contact, thundered upon hearing the word "home" leave her lips.

Chapter 11

THE ATMOSPHERE HUMMED WITH unexpected energy as we entered the inn. At this hour, I'd anticipated an empty common room, however multiple clusters of people were sprinkled throughout the tight space. The cozy room was bustling with activity, patrons engaging in lively conversation and laughter.

I exchanged a glance with Sylvane. With this amount of people, finding a vacant room seemed increasingly unlikely.

As I approached the innkeeper, I couldn't help but notice the furrowed lines etched deep into his brow. Dark-brown hair was swept back from a tan face, and hazel eyes darkened as they glanced between us. He seemed too young to look so stressed. "I'm terribly sorry," he began, his voice trembling as he darted a nervous glance in Sylvane's direction. "We're mostly booked for the night. It's fairly common the week following such a large festival."

"That's alright," I assured him. As long as he had *something*. From what Garrick had told us, this was the only inn on this side of town. "We'll take whatever you have available."

Once again, his gaze drifted to Sylvane. "It... My family's inn is humble. Not the quality you must be used to."

I relaxed once I realized that he was only nervous about disappointing her, and not her actual presence. Sylvane leaned in, as if imparting a secret, her eyes twinkling with mischief. "I once spent an entire season sleeping out in the dirt under the stars on a bet. I can guarantee you this will suit my needs just fine."

Would I ever have enough time to learn everything about her? How could you ever hope to hear centuries' worth of stories without feeling lacking in comparison? I didn't know, but I wanted to try. I wanted to know it all.

"I have one room left," he admitted. "It was reserved for a couple that decided to return home early. If you'd like to take it..."

Sylvane looked as if she were about to agree before she hesitated and turned to me. I gave her an encouraging nod, taking a step closer.

"Yes, I... Alright. I'm pretty sure it's ready." The man slunk out from behind the table. We followed behind him as he took us through winding corridors lit by arcane lanterns. The walls were lined with rich tapestries and wooden paneling, and the air was fragrant with the subtle scents of smoke and cedar.

He stopped at the door to a room nestled at the far end of the hall and ushered us inside. A crackling fire already danced in the hearth, bathing the entire room in warm, flickering light, and two plush armchairs sat enticingly before it. It was better than anything I'd pictured. The only thing that gave me pause was the single bed in the center of the room that seemed just spacious enough to accommodate two. It was what he'd implied when he'd mentioned it was a single room, and yet...

Behind me, I could hear Sylvane thanking him graciously, offering him payment and requesting that two of tonight's meals be sent up before he took his leave. Then the door shut, and it was just us.

"I'm glad we didn't bring our own provisions," she said, collapsing into one of the armchairs. "Can you imagine how inedible they would seem right about now compared to hot stew?"

I chuckled, setting my things on the bed behind her and using her distraction to strip out of my dirty clothes and into my soft, cream-colored shift. It was only after I'd tugged it down the length of my body that I realized I would have to sleep next to her in it. The indecency made my cheeks pink. What if she'd wanted me to stay in my clothes from earlier?

It was too late to change my mind as she was already standing, arms raised over her head in a big stretch. She froze when she saw me, arms lowering almost unconsciously. Her golden eyes raked their way down my body, stopping when they reached the hem of my dress, which to my knees. I fought the urge to cover myself up somehow, fully aware that I was turning scarlet. It felt utterly scandalous to be standing before her in such a state.

"You're breathtaking," she said in a low voice.

My gaze dropped down to the wooden floorboards. No one had ever said such a thing to me before. I felt as though I owed her some honesty in return. "I wish you could stay," I whispered. She didn't react, inscrutable eyes scanning me as I continued. "I like your company. I... I like *you*."

"I like you too," she murmured, taking several confident steps forward until she was standing before me. "I didn't put any thought into what I might sleep in, and ended up bringing nothing but a change of clothes for tomorrow. Do you have any ideas?"

I can do this. I can absolutely do this.

"Nothing?" I said in a rush. When she grinned approvingly, her sharp eye teeth flashing in the firelight, I repeated it again with more confidence. "Nothing."

"Would you like to do the honors?"

"That seems a little advanced," I responded weakly, grinning when she threw her head back with a laugh.

"You're right, little witch, but I have faith in you. Even so, I'll take it easy on you this time."

This time?

She didn't draw it out, pulling the tunic over her head along with the band over her breasts, then stepping out of her trousers with a swift impatience, leaving her completely bare.

Shock and admiration held me in their clutches as my gaze traveled over every curve of her body. Dark-silver hair cascaded over creamy skin, the flowery scent that clung to her growing stronger by the second. Her waist sloped inward, flaring out near her hips and then dipping once more. Small scars decorated her body, and there were little clusters of freckles that I had the strangest urge to trace with my tongue.

I never wanted to look away.

"Like what you see?" she asked, voice quiet and beckoning like a siren's call.

"Yes," I breathed, tentatively extending my hand to brush the length of her hair back behind her shoulder, exposing the entirety of her perky breasts and rosy, peaked nipples. Keeping my eyes on hers, watching her eager nod, I leaned forward, drawing the tip of one into my mouth before pulling back to tease her with just a lick. Blood rushed to my head so quickly that I feared I might collapse.

Her gaze on mine heated with arousal and a touch of surprise. While I was shy in some aspects of my life, I knew my desires. And right then, they were telling me to take her into my mouth with all of my inexperienced enthusiasm before the opportunity passed me by and she was gone once more, somewhere I would never be able to reach her.

Putting that into action, though... "I-I don't... I've never..." I couldn't seem to stop stammering, so I just closed my mouth instead.

If I thought she would be put off by my inability to string a sentence together, I would've been sorely mistaken.

"Never what?" she prompted gently, eyes falling on the exposed slope of my shoulder where the sleeve of my nightgown had fallen. Her eyes had turned a golden honey shade from the flames, like they'd been drenched in sunlight, but there was an inner glow to them as well.

I swallowed thickly. "Never done anything like this. I haven't... I—" Why was it so difficult to put into words? That before her, I'd lived without this intense longing, without ever having experienced the quickness of breath or intensity of emotion that came with the desire ignited just by her presence. Never before had I felt so woefully unprepared. "I've never been attracted to anyone like I am you. I've never missed its absence before now, because it was simply never there. I've never looked at someone and felt the urge to touch and be touched. But you..."

She looked at me in awe, soft lips parting as her eyelids grew heavy. "Attraction," she whispered. "Desire. Lust. For me? Only me?"

I nodded, and her answering smile was small.

"A gift," she whispered. "And I will treasure it. I'm honored." Sylvane lowered her head and released a soft sigh when her lips finally met mine. It was *everything*. All the fear that I might not enjoy the sensation vanished the moment sparks exploded behind my closed eyelids. Something bright and fizzy curled its way around my heart when she slid her hand around to the back of my head to hold me in place. My lips parted on instinct, and she took that opportunity to trace her tongue along my bottom lip, dipping into my mouth when I made a soft noise of encouragement. Her slick tongue twined artfully around mine, tracing the contours of my mouth with a practiced skill. It was nothing like I'd ever imagined. I'd watched couples kissing in the past, wondering what about it was so appealing, how they could look so consumed in one another when the act itself seemed so messy, but I understood the appeal now.

The scent of honey and wildflowers surrounded me in a dizzying cloud as her body pressed closer to mine. I hesitantly slid a hand up and around her waist, groaning quietly at the curve of her body, her warm skin under my hand.

Looking to me for permission first, she slipped my shift up over my head and draped it over the armchair, leaving me shockingly nude. I was paler than her, with more padding to my curves and stomach, and faint lines along the sides of my abdomen, yet her gaze devoured me like she couldn't see a single fault.

Bending down to press a soft kiss to my neck, she took my hand in her grasp and led me to the bed. I slid in after her, my hair a dark halo against the light pillows. She wasted no time in sliding down my body, nipples dragging against my skin as she moved, making my head spin. Catching my gaze with a clear intent, she parted my legs slowly enough for me to object and made a soft, wondrous sound at what she found. I was too caught up in the rapturous expression she wore to feel very self-conscious.

"You're already slick," she observed.

Heat rushed to my face at her phrasing. Not wet or damp, but slick. A lone finger trailed down my center, rubbing teasingly at that wetness before switching to my thighs, pressing soft kisses to the skin there.

I rocked my hips into her touch, desperate for her to move back after her brief preview, my hands fisted at my sides as I resisted the urge to beg. She wanted to explore, and I wanted to oblige her.

"Sylvane," I groaned through clenched teeth, and she laughed softly from where she'd been lavishing attention to the inside of my knee, fingertips circling the apex of my legs before slowly breaching my cunt, then slipping out to trace me once more.

Her other hand trailed up to pluck at my nipples, withdrawing to grasp at the soft skin of my thigh when one particularly bold touch prompted me to try closing my legs.

"Sensitive?" she asked, head tipping up to watch me with a mischievous grin. Golden eyes danced with mirth, and her cheeks were flushed a pretty pink.

A gasp escaped me. "You know I am."

"Impatient too," she tutted. Though she spared me any further torture and slipped her lithe finger all the way back inside me. Almost immediately, it crooked, rubbing at the walls of my channel until she reached a spot that made my breath quicken. Her eyes flicked up to meet mine again, and I saw the instant she plotted her next move. Glowing hair surrounded her face in a curtain as she leaned down to drag her hot, wet tongue through my center.

I threw my head back, unable to watch any further, more focused on staying in the moment and not allowing the pleasure to carry me away. At her urging, I threaded my hands through her silky hair to capture her head, holding it to me firmly and occasionally tracing the pointed shells of her ears. She made a pleased noise of assent, her tongue working in deep strokes and pointed licks to manipulate the bundle of nerves I'd only tried to stimulate on a handful of failed occasions, only this time the sensations were euphoric.

It was noisy in the room now, loud moans and wet sounds echoing off the walls, pants and mewls slipping from my lips as she worked. When I craned my neck forward to watch her once more, I could see her hips moving just out of view as she worked herself over, humping her own hand just out of sight. It was that view that tipped me over, and I came with a shocked cry, pleasure seizing my body in waves. Stars danced behind my eyes as I sank into the bed, incapable of speech. I clenched rhythmically down on her fingers, shuddering wildly as she drew the feeling out as long as she could.

After taking a moment and a spare corner of the blanket to clean us both, she settled beside me, hesitating as if she were deciding something.

My eyes flew open. "Oh," I slurred. "You. Your turn."

She made a low noise and shook her head. "I'm satisfied," she whispered. "Your pleasure was more than enough for me to reach mine." When she gestured for me to come closer, I did, resting my head on her damp chest like I'd done it a million times before and tangling my leg with hers.

One discreet peek at her face revealed her to be watching me softly, affectionately, like I was dear to her. It was reassuring to know that she might feel the same. Maybe things didn't have to end horribly after all.

Chapter 12

WE HAD ONLY BEEN back in Mythshaven for a day, and already things were different. Or maybe *I* was different. Despite the new knowledge of a broader world beyond our village, a comforting sense of belonging washed over me upon our return. There was a deep-rooted contentment in being back among the familiar sights and sounds of home, no matter how long I'd existed on its outskirts.

Meanwhile, Sylvane seemed to be weaving her own magic among the villagers, her presence garnering curious glances and warm smiles alike. She drew people to her with her charm and kindness, able to converse with most anyone. As we walked through the village to meet Isa and Isolde, I couldn't help but notice the change in the villagers' attitudes toward her. Some approached with genuine interest, eager to engage in conversation, while others seemed to avert their gazes, as if unsure how to react to the presence of a deity among them.

One thing that was entirely different was their behavior toward me. There were no longer any judging whispers or sidelong looks. I was able to walk to my destination just like anyone else, a novel experience for me. Even stranger, I was periodically stopped for questions about my services. Could I alleviate the pain from a sprained ankle? And what could I do for a child that wouldn't stop coughing? What about a sore throat or issues with fertility? It was endless, and not unwelcome.

There was an undeniable undercurrent of positivity in the air, as if Sylvane's presence had breathed new life into the village, and with it a large dose of tolerance.

Loud laughter caught my attention, and I frowned, watching as a younger woman wearing a fitted dress flirted with her husband. I tried not to let trivial things bother me, but curiosity was devouring me slowly, doubt whispering in my ear every time Sylvane glanced my way since our night together.

She shot me a questioning glance, easily noting that something was wrong. I sighed, deep and long, knowing that she wouldn't let me get away with pretending it was nothing. "I just don't understand. I'm... older. And..." I looked down at my body, the generous padding to my hips, the cushion to my stomach, and the way my thighs brushed together while I walked. I knew it was just the way my body was made, but I'd have to be oblivious not to see how I differed from the woman across the cobblestone path.

Sylvane reached out slowly, like there was a chance her touch wouldn't be welcome. I must've made a face, because her lips turned up at the corners and she lightly trailed her hand across my hip before anchoring it to my side. The other came up under my chin to gently tilt my head back, moving my gaze from my feet to her face. Stars above, she was enchanting. It struck me as brand new every time I saw her.

"I have walked this land for centuries," she murmured, those otherworldly, honeyed eyes landing on mine to hold them captive. The seriousness in her stare froze me in place. "I've seen old, tall, short, large, small; all variations of the mortal form, and I have found a unique beauty in every one. And you, my little witch..." Her sigh was a balm to all the parts of me I hadn't realized were aching. The desire in her eyes as she ran them down my body was too palpable to be faked. "You are exquisite. These things you speak of, they mean nothing to me. I see you, and your soul, and your softness, and I find you to be everything I have ever wanted. And your eyes... like spring leaves. I've never seen such a stunning shade of green."

I drew a sharp breath at her honesty, at the depth of her feelings, watching as her gaze turned wistful. "I should like to wear my age one day. Smile lines from happiness and crow's feet from wisdom. Besides"—she laughed, the joyful sound drawing eyes from all around the square—"one and thirty is not old, Elise." I laughed, leaning up onto the tips of my toes to press a kiss to her lips, mouth curving into a smile when she chased after me even once I was firmly back on the ground. She slid her hand from my hip to my arm, tracing my skin until she reached my hand and laced it with hers. This easy affection was new, and so very welcome. I couldn't imagine ever going without it. The thought of her impending departure threatened to sour my mood, and so I tried to think of other things. Like how cute Silas had looked that morning, curled up on Sylvane's lap while we ate breakfast.

We reached Isolde's home just as the sun had begun its slow descent beyond the horizon. The interior was tidy and organized, lacking in the personal effects that littered the rest of our homes. She was the only one of us who could live so neatly, all her belongings tucked away in their own designated spots. The walls were a dark red shade, matching the dark-colored wooden antiques she'd placed throughout her home. The entire space had a regal feel, and the sweet scent of desserts drifted throughout the house, telling me that Isolde had been stress-baking earlier.

Isa was already there, sprawled out in one of the armchairs. Sylvane and I took a seat on the blue velvet settee in front of her. The only reason we'd waited so late was because Isa couldn't leave until my father arrived to watch the kids, and he'd been busy earlier in the day. While we could have met at her house, we didn't want to have to moderate our volume.

Isolde returned, taking a seat in the chair to Isa's right, which meant Sylvane and I could begin explaining what we'd found in Elmspring. Our audience listened with rapt attention, injecting questions that grew increasingly difficult to answer.

"So the likelihood of it being at another temple is slim to none," Isa said once we'd finished, coming to the same conclusion as we had the other day. She looked radiant, round cheeks glowing and hair tamed back in a low ponytail. The news that Finn would be returning in several weeks had probably given her a much-needed boost of energy. I would've done anything to keep her that positive all the time instead of the more reserved version of herself she became under stress.

"Yes," Sylvane confirmed. "We plan to do more re—" She stopped mid-sentence, head cocking to the side in an eerie imitation of a predator stalking its prey.

I froze, listening intently for whatever had caught her attention. Isa and Isolde seemed to catch on, both going silent as they watched Sylvane. It was then I heard a muffled curse coming from the kitchen. Isa's eyes widened, but Sylvane just huffed loudly and rose from her seat.

"Must you intrude, brother? There are rules about this sort of thing."

A man walked into the room from the kitchen, mouth working, presumably from the tartlet he held in his right hand. The resemblance to Sylvane was impossible to miss. His presence commanded attention, if only because of his predatory features. Sharp teeth peeked out from beneath a mischievous smile above a pointed chin, and unlike Sylvane's silvery hair, he had dark-green locks that framed his face, cascading in waves that ended at his ears. They shared the same eyes, though—an otherworldly liquid gold.

It was strange to see the god that I had been raised to honor in the flesh. Unlike the other deities I worked with, I never called upon him for spell work or divination, only performing the duties of my line and making sure he had regular offerings and prayers. He felt unfamiliar to me, so close to being a stranger, yet not.

Isolde made a shocked sound, but one look at her expression revealed it to be anger and not fear. Pale skin flushed red as she stared at the dessert in his hand. She wasted no time in voicing her displeasure, her words slicing through the air. "You can't just barge in here and raid my kitchen, especially for something that took all day to make and used the last of the wildflower honey! I don't care who the hell you are," she chided, stretching to her full height and still only reaching his shoulders.

The god had no way of knowing that my older sister had a deep, secret passion for baking. She could spend the entire day in the kitchen on occasion, and didn't mind handing them out when she had extra. That he'd taken one without asking was a grievous offense in her books.

His grin was much sharper than Sylvane's when he tipped his head down to examine her, the entire move reminiscent of a crow. "Oh? And what do we have here? A prissy little mortal, it seems."

She damn near bared her teeth, something she hadn't done since before her teens. "I'm not little," she bit out. "And I'm not prissy. Just an observer of propriety and politeness."

He laughed, his smirk growing as those otherworldly eyes fell half-mast, turning him even more predatory somehow. How she could stare up at him so fearlessly, practically drilling her finger into his face, was an endless source of amusement to me, if not also a little frightening. Who was to say when it would stop being a game to him and turn into something that would earn consequences? "Such big words for a prickly little porcupine."

Sylvane jumped in before Isolde could attempt to seriously injure him. "Enough, Thorne. Stop antagonizing my friends."

"Friends?" he remarked, biting off another piece of the tartlet in his hand despite Isolde's frustrated growl. "With mortals?"

"Must you?" She sighed. "Why are you here?"

"My sister finally came out of her self-imposed exile. How could I not want to see her?"

Sylvane scoffed, but I wasn't so quick to assume he was joking. He watched her with a solemn quality, like he'd actually missed her company. She threaded her hand through mine, garnering a multitude of reactions from the entire room. Isa beamed, Isolde winked, and Thorne... His jaw dropped. "With one of mine?"

"You recognize me?" I asked.

"Much as you might think otherwise, my followers are not so great as to become a faceless horde. I know you, yes. Of the Durand line. I helped you, didn't I? Showed you the information on the festival and the plant?"

I nodded, leaning into Sylvane when she made a tiny sound. Her body was so firm, just touching her sent unexpected bolts of affection and interest down my spine. His gaze dropped to our intertwined hands and turned a little less hostile, more appraising now. "I see. And you've left offerings for my twin as well. I just had to see what my dear sister was up to, whatever could be keeping her so occupied that she hadn't even thought to come visit me since waking. Now that I'm here, the answer seems fairly obvious."

My blush transformed into a full-body flush when Sylvane leaned down to kiss my cheek, the scent of wildflowers bringing me back to our night together. "I am helping Elisette with something. We only have a short time frame."

Isolde wobbled a bit where she stood, and retreated to take a seat with Sylvane and I. Thorne's gaze followed her as he moved to take the her now empty seat. "So? Aren't you going to tell me?"

While Isolde's irritation only grew, Isa just laughed. As the night advanced, I rehashed the entire situation that had led to that point. To his credit, Thorne listened raptly, eyes never once leaving my face, aside from the occasional slide in Isolde's direction whenever she made a displeased sound. If my sisters were bored from hearing the story for yet another time, they didn't speak a word.

At one point, the fire had faded to just embers, and a chill permeated the room. Isolde made to stand and stoke it when Thorne extended one long finger, and the flames roared to life once more.

I whipped my head around to face Sylvane. "Can you do that?"

"Yes..." she replied hesitantly, like that would be the final nail in the coffin of the differences between us.

"You know what this means, right? No more leaving the blankets in the middle of the night when it's freezing."

Her laugh was tinged with relief. "My little witch," she whispered, pressing a kiss to the top of my head and drawing me further into her side. I shivered, sliding a hand around to rest against the small of her back.

Isolde finally looked away from the hearth, and Thorne's gaze followed her once more. "So," he said. "You have a little over a week left to find the plant or your father loses his land. This doesn't sound like the end of the world to me."

I winced when Isolde snapped, "We grew up in that home, paid it off with blood, sweat, and tears. Cultivated crops on the land and raised livestock that produces things my father takes to the market now that he can no longer woodwork. You'd have my father go hungry? He's not just losing *things*. He's losing his livelihood. His last connection to our mother. Besides, what kind of world is this where he gets punished for saving Callum's life?"

To my surprise, and evidently Sylvane's when she made a small sound, Thorne capitulated with a nod. "Very well. I didn't mean to imply... That is... I understand. Either way, I'd like to offer my assistance."

Sylvane broke the tense silence with a sigh. "You were bored, weren't you."

"And what if I was? Things have changed. The other gods are no fun anymore. Besides, I only have one sister. How could I not wish to spend time with her?"

"I think with their idea of fun, that that's a good thing," she said dryly. "And don't try to pull the sister card on me when you're the same one who hid my scythe for a century."

"Oh, don't be so uptight." His grin was all teeth, sharp and deadly. "You never needed it, anyway; it was an accessory."

"Hang on. You're both gods of agriculture. Why can't you just magic up the plant we need?" Isa interjected. I was proud of my baby sister for feeling brave enough to speak her mind. I knew if it was possible, Sylvane would have already mentioned it, but I was also eager to learn why.

"That's not within our capabilities," Sylvane explained gently. "With every year that passes, every day we're not walking among mortals and inspiring faith, our powers grow weaker. Though they were never capable of summoning something from nothing."

"Then what are you good for?" Isolde huffed, glaring at Thorne.

"Isolde!"

She crossed her arms and leaned back in her seat. "Fine, I'm sorry."

"Is he going to curse her or something awful?" I whispered to Sylvane, glad that he was still wearing that amused grin and didn't look as though he was about to destroy her home for fun.

"No. She intrigues him far too much. Though a little mindfulness never hurts."

"Oh?"

"Mortals used to caution that interacting with Thorne was like bargaining with the fae. Best done with caution and scarcity, but even better, not at all. He's had a lot of years to grow into his indifference and he wears it like a cloak."

I shuddered, watching as Isolde turned her nose up in his direction before moving her attention to me. "So, how can we help, Elise? Time is running out."

Chapter 13

THE MARKETPLACE BUSTLED WITH activity. Shoppers browsed the stalls, their arms laden with bags and baskets filled with fresh produce and artisanal crafts. The air was alive with the sounds of chatter, laughter, and the occasional haggling. Sunlight filtered down on us, casting dappled shadows on the cobblestone paths below.

As we wove through the crowd, I caught glimpses of unfamiliar faces and goods, telling me that the amount of curious visitors who'd heard the rumors had increased once more. Maybe Esme or Ms. Wilder would have some good news for me today.

The days had melded into one another, each one a blur of activity as we struggled to find a balance. With Sylvane by my side, the mundane tasks that usually occupied my time took on new meaning. During the day, we processed visitors who stopped by to receive treatment—and, strangely enough, more arcane items like charms, as of late—and in the evenings, she and I would retire to the front room and surround ourselves with stacks of old grimoire texts and crumbling scrolls as we searched for any shred of information that might lead us to the vitalara plant.

Each night we ended up in each other's arms, a novel experience for me, and in the quiet hours of the morning before the village stirred to life, we'd steal moments together. Something about the tranquility of the predawn hours made everything feel so much more real. We would sit by the hearth, bodies fitted together like puzzle pieces, our conversations hushed and intimate as she told me stories from her past or the origins of some of her myths. She asked me about my mother often, proclaiming that the life advice she'd given me was invaluable, and that she must've been very wise.

But it wasn't just in the quiet moments that Sylvane worked her magic. With a charming smile and many, *many* compliments, she promoted my services, boasting about how effective my talismans were or how quickly I could alleviate certain aches and pains.

That wasn't all.

She'd been telling stories from her past. About magic, and how useful it had been to her and her fellow immortals. How witches, mages, and the like had been employed in every major city and town, indispensable to their communities. And didn't we know how necessary protective wards were? Everyone was using them now. Or how incredibly popular it was to possess luck charms? Everyone in the cities had them.

It was slow, and strange, but whispers of skepticism soon gave way to admiration, and once-cold stares softened into warm and genuine greetings.

For *me*. All because of her.

We passed an older gentleman with a display of tulips that looked at least several days old. Others passed by his stall without a glance, saving their attention for the brighter, fresher displays, and his tremulous smile dropped a little with each one.

I clutched my locket close, rubbing the etched surface soothingly. He reminded me of myself just a few short weeks ago. Nothing like now, where people stopped us in the street to ask Sylvane for her assistance or request an appointment with me. How things had changed... a night-and-day difference. By now it was common knowledge that the goddess was... *involved* with me, and willing to help however she could, yet the man spotted Sylvane and offered her a respectful nod, asking nothing of her.

Sylvane returned his nod, and just when I thought she would continue on walking with her hand in mine until we reached our destination, she twirled a finger. Within seconds, the flowers perked up, once more beautiful, healthy blooms looking as if they'd been picked fresh that morning. When the man realized what she'd done, he made to leave his spot, but she waved him off, quickly weaving through the crowd and pulling me along with her.

I laughed quietly at her visible distress. "What, was that so scary to you?"

"You know I don't like it when they thank me." She groaned, hands rubbing over her face. A pointed ear poked through her silver hair, and I gave it a soft stroke as I rested a hand on her waist to keep my balance as I kissed her cheek.

"You'll get used to it," I informed her, eyes searching hers for any indication of her plans. Would she stay long enough to? Had she already had enough, bored of living such a small life?

She tilted her head to the side, watching me with an unspoken curiosity. "I'm not sure I will."

Just then, Esme's voice rang through the crowd, and she waved from where she stood around the corner from the fromagerie. I carefully pushed my way through until I reached her, throwing myself into her open arms.

"Missed you," she muttered, clutching my upper arms and leaning back to get a good look at me. The sunlight glinted off her spectacles and made her dark skin glow, giving her a luminous appearance. Esmeraude's eyes widened, and I felt Sylvane at my back as she caught up. "So this is her, the famous goddess who decided to grace our town."

I grinned, happy to introduce two of my favorite people to one another. They each gave polite nods, discreetly examining the other.

"I'm glad to finally meet you," Sylvane said suddenly. "Elise speaks so highly of you."

Esme's mouth lost some of its tension. "Likewise. I heard a lot about you the other day when I ran into Elise. Seems you've been a positive influence on her reputation." She led us to the front of her parents' shop, a slightly quieter area where we weren't jostled every second. "I'm sorry to tell you that I haven't heard anything. News has spread of your arrival, Sylvane, and merchants are coming from far and wide to catch a glimpse of you, but no word of vitalara."

My heart sank. "Much as I'd hoped, I wasn't expecting to hear differently." I pulled the end of my long braid over my shoulder to twine the end around my fingers, the crowd's volume getting to be overwhelming. "Four more days, and nothing to show for it. Maybe we should've been focused on gathering money for the payment this entire time instead."

"It's not over yet," Esme assured me. "We'll figure something out. If the worst case happens, you have people who love you who want nothing more than to help. I'll keep listening, okay?"

Mrs. Dupont called her name from inside, and she pulled a sour face. "I have to go." Esme stopped and turned halfway into the shop, waggling a stern finger at Sylvane. "You look after her."

I gasped, but Sylvane threw her head back with laughter. "No question there," she declared.

WE'D GONE TO THE apothecary after visiting Esme, but Ms. Wilder hadn't heard anything either. Asking around ourselves had returned nothing but apologetic shrugs. We even passed Alden at one point, who'd withheld his trademark smirk for a much more humble expression. I had a feeling it was because of the goddess towering over me as she walked at my side.

On our way home, Sylvane stopped to help an injured mouse that lay at the side of the road, whispering quiet words to take away its pain before setting it down gently. Watching her perform magic was a sight that would never leave me. The soft glow that infused her hands and eyes, the look of belonging and rightness she wore.

She was so much more than this, than me and this small village. An immortal being with centuries of experiences. How could she want to confine herself here? A force of nature, brimming with magic and energy, with countless adventures awaiting her. So what did it matter that I needed her to stay like I needed air? To hold her back and stifle her creativity would be a crime.

A knock sounded at the door just as I collapsed into my armchair, pausing my spiraling thoughts. I hopped to my feet, wincing as they gave a pained throb, and threw open the pale-yellow door to reveal a man.

He swept his brown hair out of his eyes, looking somewhat lost as he directed nervous glances to his surroundings.

"Do you need something?" I prompted, eager to get off my feet once more.

"I'm Lucas. I... Well, I was told you had something that might help with nausea?"

I didn't know why he'd phrased it like a question, but I'd see what we could do. I led him to the kitchen, directing him toward the nearest chair when Sylvane swept into the room wearing a loose, cream-colored chemise and a flowing red skirt that was delivered the other day.

Lucas's jaw dropped, and he turned a peculiar shade of green. "So it's true," he breathed. "You have a goddess staying with you."

She introduced herself while I prepared the ingredients for an elixir, slipping past her to gather everything I needed. Her hands landed on my hips during one pass to help me move, and I had to spin and face the wall after so as not to broadcast my feelings to the entire room.

I plucked herbs from the various jars I'd set aside, and the aroma of crushed mint and chamomile filled the air, mingling with the earthy scent of dried ginger root. Sylvane handed me the peppermint oil, watching as I added several drops.

"This is to help with your nausea?"

"My wife's," he confessed. "She's been sick every morning, and mealtimes have been hard. Nothing else has worked, so..."

Sylvane beamed. "Congratulations!"

He cocked his head, wearing a small frown. "For what?"

I had to turn back around so that he didn't catch my laugh, then took a second to re-examine the ingredients with my new knowledge in mind. Sylvane wasn't so lucky, unable to stop the quiet giggle that escaped.

The liquid began to swirl and shimmer in the glass vial. I stirred the concoction clockwise, murmuring softly under my breath, then sealed the vial with a cork stopper.

"Here," I said as I handed it to him. Blunt-tipped fingers clutched it close, like it would fall and shatter at any moment.

"Thank you so much. You're not so bad, you know that? Not scary at all."

Sylvane's eyes grew unnaturally wide, but I just laughed. "Glad you think so."

Realizing what he'd said, Lucas slapped a hand over his mouth. "Sorry. So sorry. Thank you, though. Anything to make my wife feel better."

"You can let her know that it's a non-toxic formula, safe for all living beings."

He nodded, and if he was confused by my roundabout efforts to get my message to his wife without spilling the beans, he didn't indicate it.

I escorted him to the door, closing it behind him after listening to another litany of gratitude. Finally I was able to drop onto the settee with a heavy sigh, pleased at the sounds of the coins jingling in my skirt pocket.

"My beautiful witch." Sylvane sighed, leaning her head in her hand. "I could watch you do that all day."

I couldn't help but laugh. "Awfully boring, don't you think?"

Her eyelids lowered to half-mast as she unfolded herself from her seat with an inherent grace. I watched her hips swing as she approached, skirt twirling around her long legs. "Never boring," she murmured, lowering herself onto my lap. I sucked a sharp breath in, hands landing on her waist to grip her tight. Her cheeks were flushed, her blush the color of the coral buttercups that still grew in my mother's garden. Though she'd never known how the buttercups had gotten there, she'd always refused to remove them. No matter how much territory they claimed in other areas in the village, with her guiding hand and a touch of magic, they'd some-how stayed in their little section of her plot.

"Is that so?" I groaned, pressing my face against the crook of her neck and inhaling her scent.

Sylvane's hands trailed down my arms, back arching when my lips drifted from her shoulder to her chest, pulling aside the fabric of her blouse to reach more of her skin. Her body was a comforting weight in my lap, warm and pliant as she explored me as well.

It took me a second to realize she was whispering into my hair. "I could do this forever."

"Why don't you?"

The words left my mouth before I could even think about their effect. I stiffened, refusing to meet her questioning gaze. She gave me no choice, though, hand cupping my face to tilt my chin in her direction. This wasn't helpful. I needed to focus on the deadline, not on my impending heartbreak. It was foolish of me to indicate that I wanted her to stay here with the knowledge that I would be holding her back from better things and bigger adventures. Never mind the fact that she would say no, anyway.

"Elisette..." Hazy gold eyes held mine captive, and as she thought over her next words, her thumb rubbed small circles on my cheek.

I couldn't bear to hear the outcome. "It's fine, just forget it." When I bucked my hips to try to stand, she didn't move one bit. "Sylvane, please."

"Why are you so uncharitable toward yourself and your life? I *like* it here with you." She huffed, tucking silver hair behind pointed ears as she leveled me with a frustrated stare. It was rare for her to get upset, even rarer for her to gather her thoughts instead of thinking aloud.

"I—"

She pressed a finger to my lips, cutting me off. "I can't think of the right way to say this, but clearly waiting for the perfect words would be more of a mistake than giving you any at all, so I will tell you now. I enjoy your company. I love your quiet life. Your cottage and Silas, your village and your family. Spending time with you, living with you, has been an unforgettable experience. The way you make sure I don't want for anything, how you care for others, your kindness and beauty and humor. I could spend forever at your side hoping you might love me as I do you, but it seems I may not need to."

Gently sweeping aside the finger at my lips, I took her hand in mine and pressed a kiss to the center of her palm, blinking rapidly to stave off tears. "I don't want to stifle you," I said quietly. "I would never want to hurt you by keeping you somewhere you couldn't flourish."

"This *is* my happy place, silly little witch. What seems stifling to you seems just right to me. A cozy life, surrounded by love and affection. What more could I want? What gave you this idea that I need more?"

"You have so many stories... so many myths and legends. How could I stop you from making more?"

"I didn't have a *home* then. But I'd like to, and I'm thinking it could be here. With you. Besides, who says you can't come with me on the occasional adventure?"

A quiet sob escaped me. I dropped my head forward onto her chest, hiccupping when her arms surrounded me in a tight hug. All my life, I'd felt like I didn't belong; too *other* for the villagers, too different to be like my sisters, yet this goddess before me somehow felt the same deep longing as I did. For *me*. "Then stay," I said. She was still in my grip, so I repeated myself, voice growing stronger with each word. "Please stay. I do love you, and... I need you here with me."

"Ah, Elise. As if I could ever leave. Can you imagine? I would haunt this village, constantly checking in on you like a dog that's been cast out to the yard, making sure that you have everything you need and leaving odd gifts everywhere, like that leaf I dropped on your face once."

"I didn't know that was you." I snorted out a laugh, leaning back to rub my tears with my sleeves and feeling a burst of affection when she pushed my hands aside, using her thumbs to swipe them away instead. When she finished, she pressed a soft kiss under each eye, then over each eyelid. "No more talk of leaving. This is it, the beginning of our future together, wherever it might take us. I'm all in."

Sylvane adjusted her weight in my lap, reminding me of the reason she'd first stalked over. I grinned as I kissed her neck, murmuring against her warm skin, "Agreed. All in." Her shiver was a good reward, as was her tiny moan when I moved lower.

Without a word, she maneuvered off me, then bent down to scoop me up without effort, one arm supporting my legs with the other behind my back. I squealed at first, much to her amusement, but it was a smooth trip down the hall to my bedroom. My body hit the bed with a soft bounce, anticipation mounting as she looked down at me. At my small nod, she hiked up my skirt and immediately lowered herself to the place I needed her most.

All my racing thoughts ceased the minute she buried her head between my legs. I was drowning in sensation, head spinning so fast I felt like I was outside of my body—pleasure in its purest form.

She was glorious in her attentiveness: glowing eyes and tousled hair, skin slick with sweat, wearing concern and dedication in equal measure as she met my eyes to gauge my reaction to each move. "That's my good little witch. Just lay here and let me reward you for being so fearless."

"I'll make an effort to do so more often." I gasped, neck straining as I threw my head back, following her urging to thread my hands through her thick mass of hair and hold her to me.

Her sultry laugh was music to my ears, and when I flipped us over and reciprocated the act, her moans were too.

Chapter 14

ONE MORE DAY UNTIL the deadline, and I had nothing to show for it. Isolde had already stopped by, Isa too. Confessing that I hadn't somehow produced the plant since we last spoke was painful, but the carefully hidden defeat on their faces was worse.

Surprisingly, Thorne had stuck around a lot of the day, needling Sylvane and taking my mind off things with his endless commentary. When the ache in my chest intensified, I lit the candles at each altar, performing my usual routine since I'd fallen behind as of late.

Sylvane brewed tea, and I poured out offerings for the gods who preferred it, whilst Thorne grabbed the ale and passed it to me for Velios, the god of war. He was helping me with my courage and control issues, and preferred to assist in spell work that had a kick to it. I let Sylvane pour his, though Thorne was disproportionately amused by the way Velios turned the pale liquid in his glass a red shade just because he could, as he was wont to do.

That led to Sylvane and Thorne recounting stories from when they'd fought in the thousand-day war decades upon decades ago, side by side with Velios, as his candle danced and flickered exuberantly.

We could only pass so many hours by pretending nothing was wrong before I reached my breaking point, though. Outside, the rain pattered down on the cottage, but it still seemed like what I needed compared to the stifling warmth inside.

Some of the tension left me as I exited the house and let the rain soak me, taking in the vibrancy of the trees around me, their green hues startlingly bright despite the overcast sky. The weather was an appropriate fit for my emotional state.

All I could think about was how much we were set to lose, simply because of one man's greed. My sisters and I had spent over an hour earlier recounting stories from when we were younger, like when Mama had woken us up before the sun even rose to watch falling stars on the bench our father had built just for us, or the stray dog we liked to feed that was often found playing with the goats. Early mornings and family breakfasts, loud game nights and fighting about our heights as we'd carved notches into the wall in the spare room. Time spent with Mama when she'd brushed our hair at night while she told us stories, and the murals she'd painted on each of our walls when we were still in the womb.

The first few tears that fell were indistinguishable from the rain, carving out warm paths on my cheeks. My shoulders shook as sobs wracked my body, and I clutched at my locket like it was a lifeline, the metal cool from the rain.

A sudden snap echoed in the air, like the sharp *crack* of a brittle twig. My fingers instinctively tightened around the chain, feeling the abrupt loss of tension as the weight of the locket now sat freely in my hand.

That necklace had been passed down for generations, entrusted to me by my mother... and I *broke* it? I sobbed harder, begging the stars above to fix it, knowing that they couldn't. The sight of the snapped chain was suddenly unbearable. I hurled it with all my force into the grass with a scream, then cried harder at having lost control.

I felt Sylvane before I saw her, her hand warm on my shoulder. I reached mine up to clasp hers, losing all composure when she took my invitation for what it was and plastered herself against my back, wrapping her arms around me. It was like a dam had burst, releasing weeks of dashed hopes and pent-up frustration.

She rested her head atop mine, and the scent of wildflowers and honey drowned out the earthy smell of damp earth and vegetation from all around us.

"It's okay, my love. Deep breaths." Her cool hand came up to rest on my forehead, alternating to my overheated cheeks as she wiped away my tears. She continued to soothe me, her voice low and calm as she rocked us side to side. "It's going to be alright. Everyone gets upset, and you're allowed to grieve, Elisette."

I turned to bury myself in her embrace, rubbing my face on the damp fabric of her blouse and closing my eyes when I felt her cheek rest against my hair. "I... I just—" I gasped, incapable of speech as shudders wracked my body. Great, heaving gulps of air interrupted my sobs, and I knew it was my body telling me that it was time to be done.

"We'll take care of it," she said softly. "The jeweler can fix it."

"I hope so." I sniffled, laughing quietly when she pressed a smacking kiss to my forehead and made sure the last of my tears were gone before kissing my lips.

Sylvane slipped her hand into mine and led me over to where the locket had landed. My heart sank when I realized it had fallen on one of the stepping stones, and appeared to be resting at an odd angle. "No," I groaned. "Did I scratch it?"

She hummed. "I think you did a bit more than scratch it, little witch." She plucked it from the ground and held it out to me.

"It's... open? Mama said it wasn't possible."

We both peered at it, and Sylvane used a delicate touch to prod at the front half, opening it fully. In the center was a small bundle that, when I reached to touch, sent a tiny shock traveling up my finger.

I gasped, shaking my hand out. "What was that?"

"A spell," she murmured, golden eyes narrowed as she examined it closer. "It's functioning as a seal."

"A seal for what?"

She pressed a finger against the lump, absorbing the shock and speaking several muttered sentences in a language I couldn't understand. There was a bright flash of light, and then the gap between her finger and the object disappeared.

I carefully plucked it from the locket, pulling away the little square of fabric that had been shielding whatever it was, and sucked in a breath when a seed was revealed. "What could it be?" I asked. For all my knowledge of flora and fauna, I couldn't identify most seeds just by appearance.

"Let's see." She walked around the side of the house to reach the garden, seemingly unbothered by the rain that turned her silver hair dark and soaked her clothes. Using her magic, she displaced enough earth for a small hole, set the seed inside, and packed the earth back over top.

"I don't know about you, but I'm definitely not patient enough—" I cut off when her hands began to glow, and I remembered that we *didn't* have to wait. "Forgot you could do that," I finished meekly.

She snickered. "Perks of being with a goddess, I suppose."

Nothing happened for a long moment, until something green sprouted triumphantly through the dirt, tendrils that grew bigger and wider until they formed slender stalks topped by delicate leaves that shimmered despite the awful weather. The tips of each leaf were painted a deep indigo color, and the scent of raspberries filled the air. My hand flew to my mouth, muffling the choked gasp that left me. "It can't be."

Her grin stretched. "Oh, but it is. You have gods on your side, my love."

We peered down at the vitalara.

"There's no way I'm waiting the extra day to get it to Alden," I told her. "With my luck, lightning will hit it overnight and *poof*, no more plant."

"I'm not so sure your luck is as awful as you believe, but whatever you think is best. Go put on your shoes and cloak and we'll bring it to him now."

I bolted inside, barely keeping my balance when I slipped on the rug in the front room. Silas meowed from his spot near the windowsill, and I blew him a kiss.

I could hardly believe it. The house! The land. And Isolde and Isa when they found out. Oh, and Esme would be so happy. Not to mention my father... I bounced off Thorne as I turned the corner, rubbing my head while he smirked. "Something has you in a hurry."

"Long story, need to go. Are you coming?"

"An outing? Of course."

ALDEN WAS EAGER TO grant us an audience, welcoming us inside with a twisted expression of hope. He glanced outside before shutting the door behind us. "Must be important if you were willing to bear this weather to get here."

"You could say that," I muttered, examining the interior of his home. It was exactly as I'd expected, draped in dark fabrics and expensive wood—an overindulgent display of extravagance. I could hear someone coughing upstairs, and immediately remembered the purpose of our visit. I pulled the plant from the pocket inside my cloak, not bothering to take it off. We wouldn't be there long.

He stared at me in shock, mouth opening and closing as he struggled to find words. Instead of the smug attitude I'd been expecting, he seemed relieved and a little apprehensive. "You're not tricking me?" he demanded.

I wasn't surprised his first sentence was full of accusation. I loathed the man, but I could still empathize with the dark circles under his eyes. He was an awful person, but he must really care for his mother.

"Not tricking you," I promised. "Were you? When you swore you would forgive my father's debts?"

"No," he whispered, taking the vitalara from my hands with a gentle grip. "Please... How do I use it?"

Sylvane glanced at Thorne, who rolled his eyes, then turned back to Alden with a put-upon sigh. "Use it to brew tea," she told him. Her silver hair was dark from the water and slicked back behind her ears, exposing their delicate points. Her eyes practically glowed in the dark atmosphere created by his decor choices. "A couple leaves should do. Repeat every several hours, and after the first few rounds, feel free to add things like chamomile and celestis bark."

Alden listened with an intense focus, nodding with every word that left her mouth. "I can do that," he said. "I'm—I'll go do that. *Thank you*." He sounded almost sincere, a foreign emotion to him, I was sure.

We were ushered back outside as quickly as we'd entered. As soon as the door shut behind us, Thorne turned to face me. Apparently gods were immune to the chill, because he acted as if it weren't pouring rain. "How in all the hells did you manage to find that in the eleventh hour?"

I explained about the locket, leaving out the part where I threw it, and how the seed had been hidden away inside.

"Oh," Thorne said, wincing slightly. "That thing."

I whirled on my heel to face him. "And what, exactly, does that mean?"

"I didn't leave your family with nothing, you know. What do you take me for?" he snarked, clutching at his chest dramatically.

Sylvane smacked his chest. "Explain!"

"I helped your ancestor when her husband was dying of smallpox," he answered. "I had a small debt to pay, and was due to give back some. It's the reason your line has honored me all these years. Before I left, I gave her the seed of the plant I used to save his life. It was the dead of winter, and I didn't want to risk a live one dying. She must have cast a spell to preserve it and saved it for later. Just seems like *later* was countless generations."

"Maybe my luck *isn't* so bad," I murmured. I was almost sad to give the vitalara away. It was such an incredibly useful plant, and its presence would have prevented this entire situation from happening in the first place. "What are we going to do next time someone gets sick? Beg him for leaves?"

Sylvane slipped her hand into mine and winked at me, her little fangs peeking out behind her smile. "I think we'll be alright."

Epilogue

The sun dipped below the horizon, casting hues of orange and pink across the village square that was filled with revelers for our annual Thaloria Festival—this time actively performed in Sylvane's name like it had been years ago. She'd already told me the rush of energy it had generated within her was like nothing else. Decorations once more lined the streets, lanterns already lit for the night, and garlands hung. Music filled the air, a lively melody played by musicians that were just to the side of the roaring bonfire.

I stood at my stall, adorned with colorful banners and flowers that my niece and nephew helped apply, filled with an array of witchy wares and herbal remedies. Over the past year, I'd honed my craft, perfecting my spells and recipes with Sylvane's help so that they were fit to be sold, and earning enough goodwill that people went out of their way to greet me. Now, as I watched a young girl join her friends after asking me countless questions about what each object on the table did, I couldn't help but feel a bone-deep sense of accomplishment.

I'd woken one morning to the empty plot in the garden filled with vitalara. It turned out Sylvane had clipped a part of the plant before we gave it to Alden, then used it to create an entire patch of them. Not only that, but she'd saved several of their seeds, just in case.

We'd gone from making a modest living to lucrative overnight, selling potions, tonics, and elixirs, all laced with the plant. News had spread quickly that the plant once thought to be extinct was available again, and people traveled far and wide to purchase it. With such a large influx of people giving their business to the village, the council no longer needed half the members that they'd kept for monetary purposes, and now had an entirely different face, funding new projects and implementing experimental arcane inventions. The best part was that after Alden was politely asked to step down, he took his mother and left for one of the bigger cities to the west.

Sylvane appeared at my side, a twinkle in her eye as she extended her hand. "Dance with me?" she asked, her voice soft and inviting. I nodded, a smile spreading across my lips as I took her hand in mine. Esme, finally free to enjoy the festivities now that her family had hired several new workers, took my seat.

We moved to a spot with less people, starting slow and working up to twirls that took me off my feet and had me bent over with shocked laughter. With each careful dip and spin as the evening darkened to night, I felt every second of contentment from the last year with her, wishing on the falling star that just streaked across the sky that it would last forever.

A purple-breasted silverwing perched on a nearby lantern post and chirped at me, and I offered a silent thanks to Deeara. Because of Sylvane's missed presence, deities and immortal beings now stopped by regularly to catch up with her, bringing more magic and popularity to the village than I could've ever dreamed. I was no longer an outlier, no longer the last witch here. An arcane shop had even opened up on the main street, directing business my way when needed and trading supplies when we ran low.

As we danced, I caught glimpses of familiar faces in the crowd. Isa and her husband stood nearby, their arms wrapped around each other as they watched their children dance. We'd managed to convince Finn to stay for good after he'd arrived home to find our family's financial situation entirely transformed. Jobs had increased to meet the new demand, and because he no longer needed to travel so far to support his family, he was able to get a quieter and less dangerous job working with the metalsmith. Isa was ecstatic to finally have him around all of the time, and he was entirely devoted to her, still sending her besotted smiles when she wasn't looking.

Thorne and Isolde were beside them, bickering as usual. Once Sylvane informed Thorne of her intent to stay, he'd agreed that this seemed a good village to become the patrons of, egotistical god that he was. He'd settled in and rented himself a room at a small place just outside the village, near the crossroads. Aside from the occasional trip, he spent most of his time bothering Isolde as she went about her day and helping the occasional villager while pretending it was something he'd already been planning on doing. And didn't they know that you didn't thank someone for doing something they were going to do anyway? Coaching him to accept gratitude gracefully was a work in progress.

Isolde put all her weight on her cane and smacked the tall god on his shoulder with her free hand, missing the hungry look he sent her way when she turned her back on him and the baring of his teeth at the man who'd started to approach her.

"Who taught you to dance?" Sylvane asked, brushing my hair from my face where it had stuck on our last turn.

"My father." I looked at where he danced with Ms. Wilder, laughing louder than he had in years as he gave her a small spin.

Sylvane grinned. "The man has talent. He has her clutching her pearls already."

I barked out a laugh, elbowing her gently. She used the move to catch my arm, dipping me back so far I thought I might fall entirely. Silver hair cascaded down over her shoulder and fell in a veil around my face, hiding us from the crowd. "My dear heart," she murmured. "How I love you."

"My goddess," I whispered back, kissing those inviting, pink lips and closing my eyes when they parted.

The festival continued late into the night, a celebration of life and love and community. And as the final notes of the instruments faded into the darkness, I struggled to hold back tears at just how lucky I was, and how much I wished my mother could see me now, surrounded by so much love and acceptance.

THE BLANKETS BUNCHED BENEATH us, soft against my back and smelling of Sylvane.

She brushed a kiss against my neck, sending blood rushing to my head and making me dizzy. My breaths came a little quicker as her fingers lazily traced shapes onto my skin.

"You're so responsive," she whispered.

My eyes fluttered shut as long, elegant fingers landed in the center of my chest, stroking a soft path up and down my torso. I turned my head to the side, eyes cracking open to land on her face. She looked... not as controlled as her voice would have had me believe.

Pink colored her cheeks, darkening her starry spray of freckles. Her lips were soft, parted—untouched yet by me—but her eyes had darkened to swirling pools of need.

"You'd have me?" I murmured, stretching my neck back for her to kiss more fully. She took instant advantage, pressing her lips more firmly and using her tongue to trace a prominent vein.

I twisted around when she pulled away to adjust to a seated position behind me, worried something had happened to upset her.

"Not to worry, little witch." She maneuvered me to face forward so that I was nestled in her embrace, my back positioned at her front. Her lap was warm beneath me, chest soft and body firm when I reclined against her. Cool hands came up to clasp my shoulders, drawing me back more firmly.

"My goddess," I whimpered. My head dropped back against her shoulder, rolling to eye her neck hungrily. Unable to resist, I blew a cool rush of air toward her skin, lips curving at the small, surprised gasp that escaped her.

One hand slipped over my shoulder to venture down my front as she briefly palmed one breast.

I didn't dare plead. If she wasn't in a magnanimous mood, the teasing would be unbearable.

Her laugh was nothing but a huff of air, but I still felt it against my hair. My patience was rewarded when her hand began gently kneading and manipulating, her thumb sweeping over my nipple in back and forth motions to stimulate it further. With my body curved against her as it was, my chest was raised upward in a lewd display that made my cheeks heat.

Eager to please her as well, I kissed the bare skin of her shoulder and neck, escalating to small nips and flicks of my tongue when her quiet noises increased in volume. Her chest rose and fell quicker beneath me, hand rucking up my tunic to expose me to the room.

"Y-yes," I groaned when her hand landed fully across my burning skin. She bent down to draw the nipple closest to her into her mouth, giving it a hard suck and parting bite before stretching back to her original position. My eyes darted down to watch it strain for more of her touch, the pink tip spit-slicked and cool from the air.

It was getting increasingly hard not to try and rush her.

Finally, a hand slithered down my front. Nails scored lightly across my stomach, a circle drawn around my belly button, my abdomen... until she cupped me fully over my skirt. My hips tilted, seeking the pressure of her touch.

"More. *Please*."

"You want it?" she breathed. "My hand on you? In you?"

"You know I do."

"Then you shall have it."

A shiver rolled down my spine when her hand lifted the waistband of my skirt, and I felt her surprised laugh vibrate against my back when she found me bare.

"Naughty witch."

"That's"—a finger slipped down to run along my slit—"little witch to you."

"You're so wet," she observed conversationally. Casually, like she had all the time in the world.

"I'm about to get wetter."

That prompted a laugh.

Her fingers finally parted me, stroking just above my bundle of nerves in tight circles before traveling down to my entrance, one long, elegant finger slipping inside. At the same time, I clasped her arm to my chest, plastering her against my breasts to anchor me.

She held me there until I was writhing in her arms, trembling with want for more as she kept it just out of reach. An expert at teasing, she was detrimental to my need for instant gratification.

I was prepared to suffer through it until it occurred to me that I didn't *have* to wait. I twisted in her grip, flipping around to pin her to the bed, albeit clumsily. Her grin was wicked and anticipatory, with an edge of affection that never quite managed to disappear.

With a steady hand, I stroked her as she had me, drinking in her sighs and gasps, the flare of her golden eyes as she tracked my movements. She was wet and tight, clutching at my fingers like she never wanted me to leave. I gave her nipples the same treatment, sucking on them as she had mine, leaving small bites across her breasts that I knew she loved looking at the next day.

"Yesss, that. Keep doing that," she groaned, hands grasping at the blankets underneath her.

I crooked my fingers inside of her and watched, enraptured, as her body responded eagerly. And when she grabbed my hips, pulling me forward so our bodies were perfectly aligned, I let her, dipping down to capture her lips in a messy, passionate kiss. The sensations had carried me away, hands roaming feverishly over all the parts of her I could reach, clutching her close like she'd disappear if I let go.

Somewhere in all this, I became aware that her long, shapely leg had slotted itself between mine while we were grinding against one another. A tiny smirk graced her mouth as she adjusted her leg so that it was several inches higher than before. I gave an experimental roll of my hips, sucking in a quick breath at the ecstasy that filled me with such a simple move.

Sylvane looked at me in invitation, biting her lip when I rolled my hips once more, speechless as pleasure consumed me. It was intoxicating; the firm yet soft skin of her thigh, the heat of her body in all the places it touched mine, the dizzying scent of *us* and the slick sound of our movements filling the air.

By her, I was undone.

I gripped her shoulders, mindlessly rocking in a steady rhythm. Sweat beaded along my temple, lips parting to gasp out each breath. Her hands assisted my hips in their movements, the sounds of our heavy breaths and whimpers filling the room, along with the swish of fabric that we'd been too preoccupied to remove. My own thigh stimulated her in much the same way as I moved, making the experience as pleasurable as possible for both of us.

It didn't take long for the drugging, rhythmic movements to drive me over the edge, and a keening moan left my throat as I climaxed, the likes of which I'd never heard before. She followed quickly after, nails scrabbling at my back as her eyes squeezed shut and she moaned, loud and low.

We laid tangled together for a long time, coming down from the adrenaline. She leaned back to press a soft kiss to my damp hair, nuzzling my skin slightly as she pulled away.

"I'm glad you stayed," I said with a sigh, watching as Silas deemed it safe once again to jump up on the foot of the bed.

"I wouldn't want to be anywhere else but here with you, with our family. I love you, Elisette. My little witch."

Every time I heard the words, they sent a rush of adrenaline to my heart that I knew would take decades to fade, if it ever did. "I love you too."

We'd talked about the future many times before—mostly in terms of what ifs and possibilities, different rumors she'd overheard through the years of mortals and their immortal lovers or deities with special gifts for longevity—but we were content to just exist for now. They were all things we could discuss in time. With Sylvane by my side, I was ready to face whatever the future held.

For now, I was content to just *exist* with her, in a life filled with love and family. Like she'd said, there wasn't anywhere else I'd rather be but in my warm, cozy cottage, lying in her arms as we listened to Silas trilling at something in the front room and watched the snow fall in dancing flurries outside the window.

Author's Note

This book was more difficult to write than I anticipated, and the initial concept had a lot more angst and action. The more I wrote, the more it wanted to stay light instead, which was a nice break from my usual books. Instead of over-developing every scene and detail so that all the logic fit in an orderly and believable fashion, I played around with impossibilities and had fun doing it. I also just *had* to watch Howl's Moving Castle, Stardust, and the 2014 version of Beauty and the Beast (not even kidding, it's playing this very second as I type this and can we talk about how beautiful the scenery is in that movie?!) among others on repeat to get the vibes right.

It's always scary to put a piece of you out into the world for everyone to see, but I've had this story drifting around my head for a while and I was determined to finally tell it. To each and every reader that spent the time to read it, whether you enjoyed it or not, I'm eternally grateful.